英語力 3

16堂流利英語聽說訓練課

Listening and Speaking in Everyday Life

作者 Owain Mckimm　譯者 丁宥榆
審訂 Treva Adams

MP3
寂天雲 APP

如何下載 MP3 音檔

❶ 寂天雲 APP 聆聽：掃描書上 QR Code 下載「寂天雲－英日語學習隨身聽」APP。加入會員後，用 APP 內建掃描器再次掃描書上 QR Code，即可使用 APP 聆聽音檔。

❷ 官網下載音檔：請上「寂天閱讀網」（www.icosmos.com.tw），註冊會員／登入後，搜尋本書，進入本書頁面，點選「MP3 下載」下載音檔，存於電腦等其他播放器聆聽使用。

CONTENTS MAP

UNIT	FUNCTION	VOCABULARY
page_ 08 **1** Talking About Learning Experiences 談論學習經驗	◆ 討論過去所學與未學 ◆ 討論你上某堂課至目前為止所學 ◆ 說明學習至今所費時間 ◆ 說明一段時間的學習成果 ◆ 討論困難和挑戰性	◆ 課程名稱 ◆ 能力 ◆ 錯誤
page_ 16 **2** Recalling Past Events 回憶過去事件	◆ 回憶到過去某個時間的人生轉變 ◆ 談論你為某件事所做的準備 ◆ 為過去行為提出解釋 ◆ 回憶導致某結果的一連串事件	◆ 不規則動詞的過去分詞
page_ 24 **3** Talking About Life Changes and Memories 談論人生轉變與回憶	◆ 談論童年回憶和習慣 ◆ 談論自童年或某一事件以來，你的人生轉變 ◆ 討論你的個性、喜好或習慣的改變	◆ 童年活動和習慣 ◆ 重大事件或改變一生的事件
page_ 32 **4** Chatting and Telling Personal Stories 閒聊與談論個人經歷	◆ 和小組分享個人故事或消息 ◆ 加入正在進行的對話 ◆ 延續和結束對話 ◆ 回應某人說的話	◆ 加入對話與跟上話題 ◆ 表示你有在聽 ◆ 表達興趣、驚訝或無法置信 ◆ 結束和開啟自己的話題 ◆ 延續一段對話
page_ 40 **5** Having an Argument 爭執	◆ 抱怨某人的行為 ◆ 針對一項控訴自我辯駁 ◆ 推卸責任 ◆ 結束爭吵	◆ 常見的控訴 ◆ 抱怨與推卸責任 ◆ 自我辯駁與結束爭吵
page_ 48 **6** Talking About Regrets 談論遺憾	◆ 為錯誤的決定感到後悔 ◆ 為過去的行為感到後悔 ◆ 為未達成的行動感到後悔 ◆ 談論事情可能如何轉變	◆ 令人後悔的行為和更好的選擇
page_ 56 **7** Relationships 人際關係	◆ 談論讓關係更好的因素 ◆ 談論維持一段良好關係的秘訣 ◆ 談論你的朋友圈 ◆ 談論兩人是否合得來	◆ 維持一段良好關係所應該／不應該做的事 ◆ 良好關係的要件 ◆ 人際關係的種類
page_ 64 **8** Learning How to Balance Your Budget 學習平衡收支	◆ 平衡收支 ◆ 存錢	◆ 賺取額外收入的方式 ◆ 花費與帳單

LISTENING	GRAMMAR	SPEAKING	PRONUNCIATION
◆ 聆聽他人的學習經驗 ◆ 辨識困難、挑戰性和錯誤 ◆ 評估一段時間以來的進步	◆ 現在完成式	◆ 談論你自己的語言學習經驗 ◆ 詢問與回答不同學習經驗的問題	◆ 助動詞（have、has、am、is、are）的縮寫
◆ 辨識兩個時間點之間所發生的變化 ◆ 談論過去犯過的錯誤、做過的準備、發生過的不幸事件 ◆ 聆聽一串未依時間順序排列的事件	◆ 過去完成式	◆ 描述一個地方隨著時間以來的改變 ◆ 說出過去奇怪行徑的原因 ◆ 將一串未依時間順序排列的事件重新排序	◆ 助動詞（had）的縮寫
◆ 互相交流兒時回憶 ◆ 辨識他人自童年以來的轉變 ◆ 描述某人於特定事件之前後有何不同	◆ used to 和 be used to ◆ used to 和 would	◆ 說明你現在和兒時有何不同 ◆ 討論你的個性和習慣的轉變 ◆ 談論自某一事件之後，你的人生有何轉變	◆ 句子的重音： Part 1
◆ 閒聊 ◆ 分享消息 ◆ 辨識對話內容	◆ 轉折語	◆ 針對各種話題延伸對話 ◆ 練習輪流發言、回應，並且延續對話	◆ 句子的重音： Part 2
◆ 和同事與親戚爭執 ◆ 聆聽控訴內容、辯駁用語和反方爭論點	◆ 使役動詞（let、have、make、get）	◆ 集思廣益想出爭執的主題 ◆ 扮演爭執的雙方 ◆ 自我辯駁、推卸責任與結束爭執	◆ 語調重音
◆ 聆聽人物談論他們的童年 ◆ 辨識遺憾之事 ◆ 預測事情的發展將有何不同	◆ 使用 if 的第三條件句（與過去事實相反的 if 條件句）	◆ 談論憾事與過去行為的結果 ◆ 請班上同學談論個人的憾事	◆ 連音
◆ 辨識兩人的關係 ◆ 記下兩人來往過程的點滴 ◆ 聆聽人物談論維繫關係的關鍵	◆ too、also、so、either、neither	◆ 談論你最要好的朋友 ◆ 討論維繫各種人際關係的要訣	◆ 對比重音
◆ 聆聽人物說明他們的經濟狀況 ◆ 留意某人的收支情形 ◆ 針對某人的財務問題提出解決方式	◆ that + 名詞子句	◆ 談論花費、存錢和平衡預算 ◆ 提供某人平衡預算的建議	◆ 音高

CONTENTS MAP

UNIT	FUNCTION	VOCABULARY
page_ 72 **9** Asking Someone Out 約會	◆ 調情 ◆ 邀某人約會 ◆ 描述自己 ◆ 拒絕他人	◆ 星座與其特質 ◆ 搭訕用語 ◆ 邀約某人
page_ 82 **10** Deadlines 截止期限	◆ 談論是否能在截止期限內完成 ◆ 預估完成時間 ◆ 協商延長截止期限	◆ 工作案件的種類 ◆ 無法如期完成的藉口 ◆ 需要延長期限
page_ 90 **11** Getting Rid of Bad Habits 改掉壞習慣	◆ 告知某人他們的壞習慣 ◆ 提供建議給有壞習慣的人 ◆ 下最後通牒要某人戒除壞習慣 ◆ 承認你有壞習慣	◆ 壞習慣 ◆ 戒除壞習慣的方法
page_ 98 **12** The Technology Craze and Problems 科技狂熱和問題	◆ 報告與解決電腦問題 ◆ 討論你的上網習慣 ◆ 描述電子產品 ◆ 談論科技的負面影響	◆ 常見的電腦問題與解決方法
page_ 108 **13** Going on a Diet 飲食控制	◆ 説明控制飲食的原因 ◆ 説明你的目標 ◆ 討論減肥方法 ◆ 談論減肥所遭遇的挑戰和挫折	◆ 體重問題 ◆ 期望的結果 ◆ 食物和營養
page_ 116 **14** Dilemmas 抉擇	◆ 衡量優缺點 ◆ 縮小選擇範圍 ◆ 詢問某人的建議	◆ 重大決定 ◆ 做出某個決定的原因
page_ 124 **15** Going for an Interview 參加面試	◆ 談論求學經歷和工作經驗 ◆ 談論你的強項與弱點 ◆ 討論工作條件（薪資、工時等） ◆ 談論你的目標與期許	◆ 工作技巧與個人特質 ◆ 常見的管理職稱
page_ 132 **16** Getting a Pet 養寵物	◆ 決定養某一種寵物 ◆ 描述寵物（品種、身世、個性等） ◆ 詢問長期照料的方法	◆ 犬貓品種 ◆ 照顧寵物

LISTENING	GRAMMAR	SPEAKING	PRONUNCIATION
◆ 調情、邀某人約會與拒絕某人 ◆ 聆聽一則邀請約會的語音留言	◆ 關係子句	◆ 角色扮演邀約某人出去約會 ◆ 使用搭訕用語 ◆ 接受約會邀請或拒絕別人 ◆ 談論你的情史	◆ 複合名詞的重音
◆ 設定截止期限並在期限內完成 ◆ 要求延期 ◆ 了解未於期限內完成的後果 ◆ 報告個人進度	◆ Take、spend、cost、pay	◆ 說明截止期限、報告進度，並提出預計完成時間 ◆ 為進度落後找藉口	◆ 母音順序
◆ 聆聽對話人物承認壞習慣 ◆ 聆聽對話人物被控訴的壞習慣 ◆ 辨識對話中提到的建議或最後通牒 ◆ 找出戒除某人壞習慣的方法	◆ 反身代名詞	◆ 控訴某人有某種壞習慣 ◆ 提出戒除壞習慣的建議 ◆ 表達你對某個習慣的感受，並對某人下最後通牒	◆ 加重音於新資訊
◆ 辨識電腦問題與解決方法 ◆ 討論上網習慣 ◆ 依據規格辨識裝置 ◆ 聆聽人物表達科技所帶來的困擾	◆ 間接問句	◆ 為電腦問題求助與提供協助 ◆ 談論你的上網活動和習慣 ◆ 向朋友描述某智慧型手機的特色	◆ 非重音字
◆ 辨識對話人物的減肥目標、罩門，以及目前的生活型態 ◆ 克服減肥的挑戰 ◆ 記錄各種減肥方式	◆ 時間連接詞：when、while、as	◆ 向夥伴描述一種極端的減肥法 ◆ 角色扮演一位節食者，說明你的目標與面臨的挑戰 ◆ 詢問與回答關於自己減肥經驗的問題	◆ 聲調界線
◆ 聆聽對話人物考慮某個決定 ◆ 留意不同選擇的優缺點 ◆ 認真考慮某個建議	◆ 關係連接詞	◆ 縮小選擇範圍 ◆ 衡量優缺點 ◆ 決定行動方向 ◆ 建議選擇某個行動方向	◆ 子音順序
◆ 聆聽某人描述求學和工作經歷 ◆ 聆聽某人表達就業目標 ◆ 辨識某人的個人特質 ◆ 辨識某人對薪資和工作條件的期望	◆ 複合動詞	◆ 扮演求職者與面試官的面試對話 ◆ 談論你的目標、薪資和工作條件	◆ 短語動詞的重音
◆ 選擇一種寵物 ◆ 依據描述辨識寵物 ◆ 詢問長期照料方式	◆ 形容詞與介系詞的組合 ◆ 片語介系詞動詞	◆ 詢問與回答關於寵物身世的問題 ◆ 從收容所認養寵物	◆ 發語音調

學習及教學導覽

《英語力》是一本什麼樣的書？

《英語力》是一本訓練英語聽力與口說能力的用書，旨在引領學生認識基礎英語會話。本書練習的編寫，皆是針對與母語人士對談時必備的英語會話，以期協助學生建立信心與理解力。

《英語力》如何協助您增進英文能力？

- 《英語力》提供了與**真實生活相符的情境和對話**，讓您與母語人士日常互動時能泰然自若。

- 本書運用生動而清楚的圖片，輔助您輕鬆學會大量的實用生字。

- 本書用清楚而簡潔的方式呈現文法要項，並提供豐富的範例。

- **大量的口語文法練習**，讓您在真實生活會話中能正確傳達訊息、避免誤解。

- 針對**文意主旨、相關細節和其他具體資訊所設計的聽力練習**，能訓練您不僅聽懂對話的梗概，也能理解更多前後文所蘊含的意義。

- 針對**關鍵片語和內文細節所設計的聽力練習**，能增進您對英文的了解，更進一步學習進階英語。

- 藉著與主題相關的各種口語練習，您將能熟練運用在本書單字、聽力、文法單元所學到的英文。

- 易懂易學的**會話範例和輔助學習的會話句型**，讓您能不費吹灰之力地自由運用在對話中。

- 透過本書大量的**兩人活動和小組練習**，您能獲得充分的口語實戰經驗。

- **豐富的圖片和建議主題**，讓您不再為了找話題而傷腦筋。

- 完善的**發音教學**單元能協助您熟悉英語的基礎發音，提供大量練習各種發音的機會，讓您的發音更像母語人士。

《英語力》是如何編排的？

- 《英語力》有 16 個單元。

- 每個單元分為六個部分。

單元結構：

I. Topic Preview 主題預覽

透過幾則簡短的會話範例，帶您進入主題。

II. Vocabulary and Phrases 字彙和片語

提供相關的字彙和片語，是您有效聽、說的重要工具。

III. Now, Time to Listen! 聽力時間！

透過各種對話、獨白和聽力練習，訓練您的聽力技巧。

IV. Now, Grammar Time! 文法時間！

正式介紹前三部分所應用的文法，並提供練習的機會。

V. Now, Time to Speak! 口語時間！

針對各單元主題，運用小組或兩人練習的方式，提供口說的練習活動。

VI. Now, Time to Pronounce! 發音時間！

每次介紹幾種發音，並提供練習讓您能認識並正確發音。

如何使用《英語力》進行教學？

- 請於每個單元的一開始，先進行 **Topic Preview** 的部分，依照**會話範例進行練習**，讓學生熟悉相關情境。同時利用這一小節來引導與主題相關的一些概念，並評估哪些概念可能較有難度。

- **介紹該單元的生字**，接著進行 **Sentence Patterns** 的教學。讓學生將學到的生字套用在句型裡，以期同時熟悉生字和句型。

- 在進行每一則聽力練習之前，先請學生**預測可能會聽到哪些生字和片語**，讓學生在練習聽力之前先有概念。

- 完成聽力練習之後，鼓勵學生挑選其中一段或數段，**再仔細聽一次，並盡量記住內容**，然後和同學一起練習會話。這是練習口語能力的好機會，也有助於他們記住常用的句型和會話模式。

- 在聽力的小節已經接觸到一些文法之後，學生對於如何使用該單元的文法結構應該已經有了粗略的概念，此時請他們**朗讀例句**，並且試著**造出自己的句子**。記得不時提問相關的問題，以確認學生是否完全理解。

- 本書的許多文法練習是必須兩兩分組進行的口語練習，為了鼓勵學生開口，在他們對話時先不要急著糾正，可以先將您所聽到的錯誤寫下來，在練習進行了幾分鐘之後才暫停，然後全班一起檢討剛才所犯的錯誤，逐一釐清學生不懂的地方。之後再練習一次，確認學生這次用對了文法。

- 本系列套書的口語練習部分，是希望藉由提供學生**大量的句型和輔助資訊**，讓他們盡量在無壓力的情況下開口說英文。如果您認為學生們已經可以自由練習了，就鼓勵他們以 Topic Preview 或者書裡任何一張圖片的情境為基礎，自由發揮對話。

- 在**發音練習**這一小節裡，讓學生先聽一次課本MP3朗讀發音，接著再聽一次，並且跟著播音員覆誦。當您認為學生們練習的差不多了，可以個別點幾個學生測試發音。

- 鼓勵學生盡量自然地唸出單字的發音，無須過度強調或加重某個特定的音。

享受學習趣！
使用新語言！
活化英語力！

ENJOY *learning!*
EMPLOY *new language!*
EMPOWER *your English!*

Talking About Learning Experiences
談論學習經驗

I. Topic Preview (001)

1 *Talking about what you've learned*
談論你已學會的事

What have you learned so far on your cookery course?

Well, so far we've learned how to make the perfect scrambled eggs and how to make French fries.

2 *Talking about the learning process* 談論學習過程

How long have you studied Japanese?

I've studied for two years altogether.

Have you ever been to Japan to study?

Yes, I studied in Japan for a few months last year.

3 *Talking about difficulties and challenges* 談論難度和挑戰性

I find keeping my balance really difficult.

Keep at it. I practiced for a long time before I could do it.

4 *Learning from your mistakes and overcoming difficulties* 從錯誤中學習並且克服困難

The first time I drove, I almost crashed!

Why did that happen?

Because I didn't use my mirrors.

What about now? Have you improved?

Definitely. I've learned a lot in a short time.

II. Vocabulary & Phrases (002)

cookery course
烹飪課

dance classes
舞蹈課

language course
語言課

singing lessons
歌唱課

driving lessons
駕訓班

chop / slice / dice
剁碎／切片／切塊

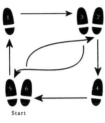
memorize steps
記下步驟

**talk about (a topic) /
pronounce new words**
談論（某個主題）／
發出新單字的發音

**breathe /
project your voice**
呼吸／發聲

**steer / use the gears /
park**
駕駛／排檔／停車

burn the food
把食物燒焦

dance out of sync
跳舞沒跟上拍子

**accidentally say
something rude**
不小心説錯話

sing out of tune
唱歌五音不全

crash 撞車

Sentence Patterns (003)

- What have you learned so far in your *dance classes*?
  So far we've learned how to *do the salsa*!
- How long have you studied *French cooking*?
  I've studied for *six months (altogether)*.
- Have you ever *studied singing*?
  Yes, I have. I *studied singing when I was younger*.
- I find *memorizing dance steps* quite difficult/challenging.
- The hardest thing about *singing* is *trying to sing in tune*!

- I need to work on *projecting my voice*.
- Keep at it! / Hang in there. / Keep practicing.
- I *studied* for a long time before I could do it.
- The first time I *sang*, I *sang out of tune*.
  Why did that happen?
  Because I didn't know how to *breathe properly*.
- Have you improved? /
  How have you improved?
  (Yes.) I've learned *how to breathe* and *control my voice*.

Now, Time to Listen!

1 Listen to Jack talk about his learning experiences. Correct the mistakes in the sentences below.

(004)

1 Jack learned how to ~~ride a motorcycle~~ when he was 17.

drive

2 Jack passed his test the first time he drove.

3 Jack almost crashed because he couldn't park properly.

4 Jack is now learning how to fly a plane.

5 Jack thinks steering is difficult.

6 Jack has been practicing how to ride for a long time.

2 Look at the topics below. Then listen to Maggie and Jim discuss their learning experiences and check ☑ what each person talks about.

(005)

		Jim	Maggie
1	What he/she has learned so far	☐	☐
2	How long he/she has been studying	☐	☐
3	Difficulties he/she is having now	☐	☐
4	Reasons for having difficulties	☐	☐
5	First-time mistakes	☐	☐
6	How he/she has improved	☐	☐

3 Listen to the following people describe difficulties and mistakes. For each one, check ☑ the pictures that illustrate their experiences most accurately.

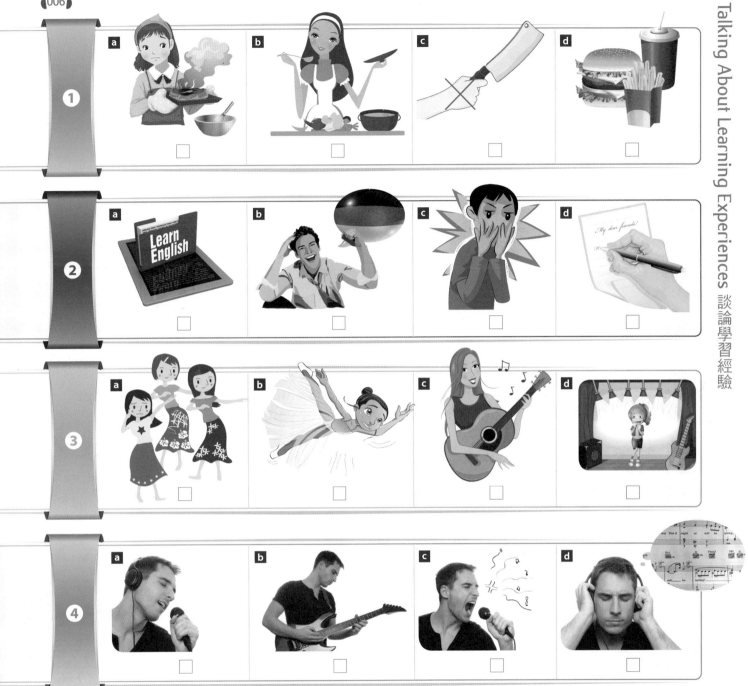

Now listen again and complete the sentences below.

1 The _____ French cooking, I _____ everything I cooked!

2 I've _____ German _____ 10 years _____, and I'm quite fluent now.

3 I still _____ dancing _____ with others very _____.

4 I need to _____ more _____ my _____ as well.

Ⅳ. Now, Grammar Time!

The Present Perfect
have / has + past participle

現在完成式：have / has + 過去分詞

Experiences 經驗	• I have studied Spanish, French, and Japanese, but I have never studied German. • Have you ever studied salsa dancing? Yes, we **have**. / No, we **haven't**.
Changes and accomplishments over time (up until now) 一段時間（直到現在）的改變和成就	• It's only the first day, and I have *already* learned how to slice, dice, and chop. • He hasn't improved much *during this course*. • What have you learned *so far*? *So far* we **have learned** how to pronounce new words.
Uncompleted actions (expecting completion) 尚未完成的動作（期待完成）	• I've been studying German for two weeks, but I *still* haven't learned how to say "hello." • He hasn't mastered salsa dancing yet, *but I think he will soon*. • Have you studied French cooking yet? No, we're going to start next week.

❹ Look at the class schedules for the adult education center. Then look at the prompts, and fill in the blanks. The first one has been done for you.

Course Name	Week 1	Week 2	Week 3	Week 4	Week 5
French Cooking	basic knife skills	sautéing	poaching	flambéing	sauces
International Dance	salsa dancing	swing dancing	tap dancing	English folk dancing	belly dancing
Oil Painting	brush techniques	perspective	light and shadow	still lifes	landscapes

1 **French Cooking, Week 3** This week the students are studying __poaching__. The students have __already__ studied __basic knife skills and__ _____. The students _____ studied _____ or _____ yet.

2 **International Dance, Week 4** This week the students are studying _____ dancing. The students haven't _____ belly dancing _____. _____ they_____ studied salsa dancing, _____ dancing, and _____ dancing.

3 **Oil Painting, Week 2** The students are studying perspective this week. They _____ studied brush techniques. They _____ haven't studied _____, still lifes, or _____.

12

The Present Perfect
have / has + past participle
現在完成式：have / has + 過去分詞

Duration from the past until now 從過去到現在的持續時間

How long **have** you **studied** English?
I **have studied** English for two years.

the past   now

study English

2 years

Usage note

When we talk about *short-term situations*, we often use the *present perfect continuous*.
討論短時間的情況時，我們通常會用現在完成進行式。
→ I **have studied** Chinese for 10 years, but I've **only been studying** Japanese for a few weeks.

5 Pair Work! Look at the pictures below. Use the present perfect or present perfect continuous to create a short dialogue.

Examples

A

Student A	How long **has** she **studied** ballet (for)?
Student B	She **has studied** ballet for **10 years**.

B

Student A	How long **has** she **been studying** ballet (for)?
Student B	She **has been studying** ballet for **two weeks**.

a study French 學法文

b work in a kitchen 在廚房工作

c ride a motorcycle 騎機車

d paint portraits 畫肖像

e do magic 變魔術

f learn to drive 學開車

6 Pair Work! Take turns asking and answering the following questions.

1. Have you studied any languages other than English?

   (*If yes*: Which other languages have you studied? What did you find difficult about those languages?)

2. How long have you been studying English?

3. What have you learned so far in this English class?

4. Do you think your English has improved? How?

5. What's the hardest thing about learning English?

6. Have you ever studied abroad? (*If yes*: Where have you studied?)

7. Have you ever made any embarrassing mistakes while learning another language?

   (*If yes*: Tell me about one of your embarrassing mistakes.)

7 Pair Work! Make a list of questions to ask the people in the pictures.
Compare your list with those of your classmates. Add any questions you don't have.

Questions
- How long have you studied French cooking?
- Have you ever made any mistakes in the kitchen?

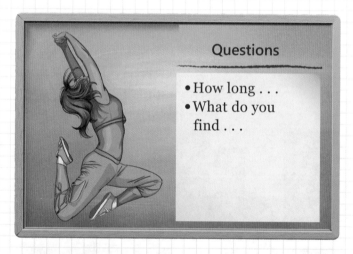

Questions
- How long . . .
- What do you find . . .

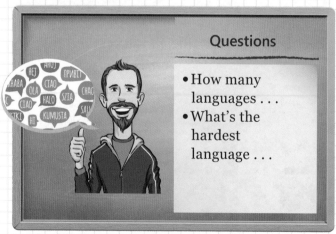

Questions
- How many languages . . .
- What's the hardest language . . .

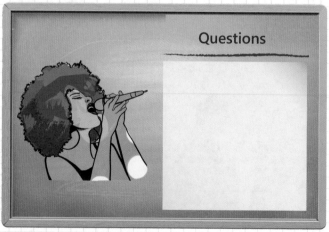

Questions

Now pretend to be one of the people in the pictures and answer your partner's questions.

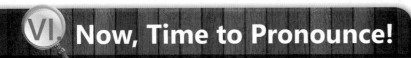

The auxiliary verbs *have* and *has* are often shortened to *'ve* and *'s* when they come after a subject pronoun.
助動詞 have 和 has 接在主格代名詞後面時，經常簡寫為 've 和 's。

8 Listen and repeat the phrases that you hear.

(008)

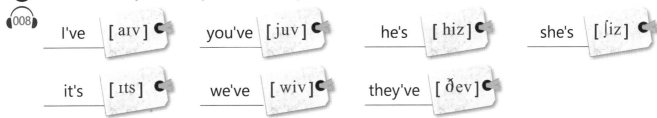

I've [aɪv]   you've [juv]   he's [hiz]   she's [ʃiz]

it's [ɪts]   we've [wiv]   they've [ðev]

(009) Now listen to the words on the right and circle the one that rhymes with the word on the left.

1	she's	peas	pits
2	they've	waif	cave
3	I've	life	five
4	it's	sits	meets

5	we've	grief	leave
6	you've	prove	hoof
7	he's	knits	knees

The be verbs *am*, *is*, and *are* are also often shortened to *'m*, *'s*, and *'re* after a subject pronoun.
be 動詞 am、is 和 are 接在主格代名詞後面時，也經常簡寫為 'm、's 和 're。

9 Listen and repeat the phrases that you hear.

(010)

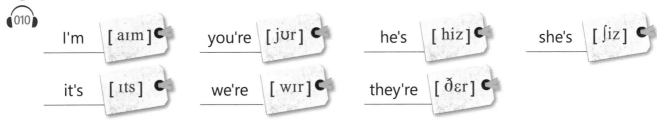

I'm [aɪm]   you're [jʊr]   he's [hiz]   she's [ʃiz]

it's [ɪts]   we're [wɪr]   they're [ðɛr]

(011) Now listen to the words on the right and circle the one that rhymes with the word on the left.

1	they're	star	stair
2	I'm	mime	slim
3	we're	care	beer

10 Listen to the following sentences. Pay attention to whether the speaker uses the full

(012) form or the shortened form of the verb. Write (F) full or (S) short in the space provided.

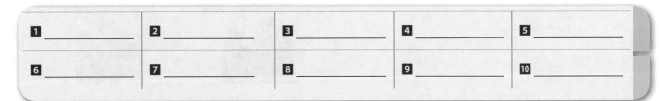

| 1 _____ | 2 _____ | 3 _____ | 4 _____ | 5 _____ |
| 6 _____ | 7 _____ | 8 _____ | 9 _____ | 10 _____ |

Recalling Past Events 回憶過去事件

I. Topic Preview (013)

1 *I didn't realize things had changed so much*
沒想到事物改變了這麼多

I visited my hometown last summer.

Oh yeah? Had anything changed since your last visit?

Yes. They had built a new hotel next to the beach and taken down the statue in the town square.

2 *Preparations, preparations, preparations*
準備、準備、再準備

Tell me about John's party last week.

OK. We'd already hidden and turned off the lights when John opened the door. Then we all shouted, "Surprise!"

3 *I can explain what happened* 我可以解釋發生的事

I saw you limping yesterday, Kim.

I was limping because I'd crashed my scooter into a tree.

You look very tanned in this photo, Brian.

Yeah. I'd just come back from a vacation.

4 *I missed something important* 我錯過重要大事

Sorry I'm late for the meeting. I forgot to set my alarm clock last night. By the time I got to the station, my train had already left.

II. Vocabulary & Phrases 🎧 014

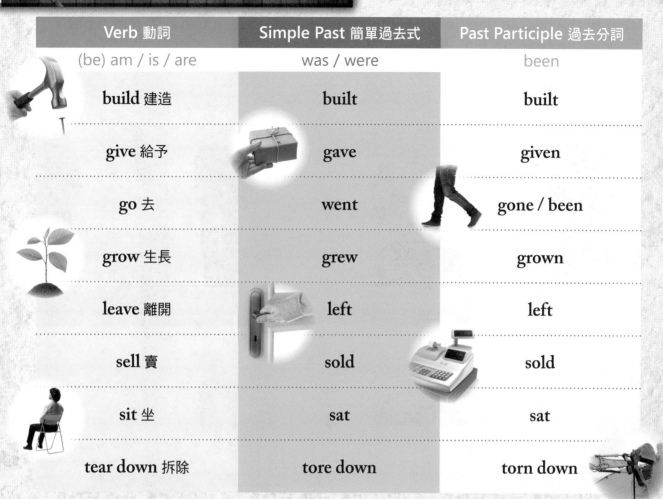

Verb 動詞	Simple Past 簡單過去式	Past Participle 過去分詞
(be) am / is / are	was / were	been
build 建造	built	built
give 給予	gave	given
go 去	went	gone / been
grow 生長	grew	grown
leave 離開	left	left
sell 賣	sold	sold
sit 坐	sat	sat
tear down 拆除	tore down	torn down

Sentence Patterns 🎧 015

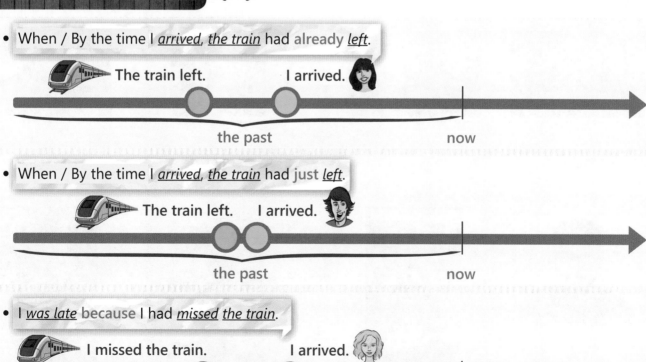

- When / By the time I *arrived*, *the train* had **already** *left*.

  The train left.   I arrived.

  the past   now

- When / By the time I *arrived*, *the train* had **just** *left*.

  The train left. I arrived.

  the past   now

- I *was late* because I had *missed* *the train*.

  I missed the train.   I arrived.

  the past   now

1 Listen to the people describe how things changed between two different times. Check ☑ the changes that occurred.

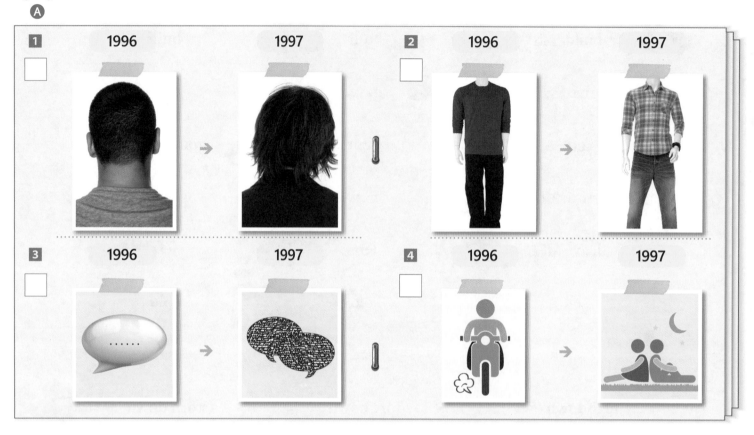

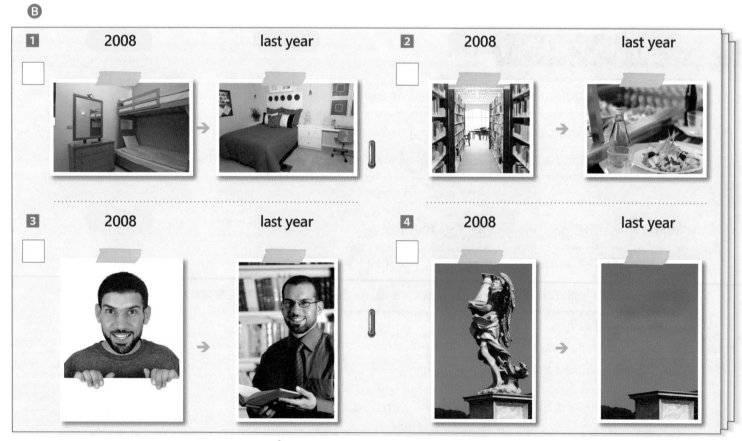

❷ Listen to the following conversations and check ☑ a, b, or c.

Ⓐ **1** Which of the following HADN'T the man done to prepare?

(017)

- ☐ ⓐ Bought a new suit.
- ☐ ⓑ Studied for a test.
- ☐ ⓒ Cleaned his shoes.

2 What had the boss done by the time the man arrived at the office?

- ☐ ⓐ Hired someone else.
- ☐ ⓑ Decided to hire the man.
- ☐ ⓒ Told everyone some good news.

Ⓑ **1** What is the main focus of the conversation?

- ☐ ⓐ Making preparations.
- ☐ ⓑ Explaining what went wrong.
- ☐ ⓒ Describing changes.

2 Which of the following is true about the beef?

- ☐ ⓐ It had gone bad.
- ☐ ⓑ Josie had enjoyed it.
- ☐ ⓒ It had been bought the day before.

Ⓒ **1** What did Mike say about the concert tickets?

- ☐ ⓐ They hadn't sold out yet.
- ☐ ⓑ He didn't know if they'd sold out or not.
- ☐ ⓒ They'd sold out.

2 What had Mike already done by the time he spoke to Sarah?

- ☐ ⓐ Called the ticket office only.
- ☐ ⓑ Called the ticket office and spoken to Jenny.
- ☐ ⓒ Spoken to Jenny only.

➡ (018) Now listen again and fill in the blanks with the expressions that the people say.

Ⓐ I had _____ down outside the boss's office _____ he came out and _____ us the bad news.

Ⓑ Because the beef _____ bad. It had _____ in the fridge _____ about two years.

Ⓒ I asked her last night, but _____ I _____ to her, she had _____ them to someone else.

❸ Listen to Lisa's story. Number the events according to their chronological order.

(019)

a	b	c	d	e

_1_ _____ _____ _____ _____

The Past Perfect Tense
(had + past participle)

過去完成式：had + 過去分詞

We usually recall events using the **simple past tense**, but when we want to make clear that one or more events happened before another, we use the **past perfect**. 我們通常用**簡單過去式**來回憶一些事件，但是若要區別事件發生的先後順序，就必須使用**過去完成式**。

Ordering past events 排序過去事件	Changes and accomplishments over time (up to a point in the past) 一段時間（直到過去特定時間點）的改變和成就
• When you called me, I had *already* gone to bed. • He had not prepared *before* he went to the interview. • Had you decorated the house *by the time* he arrived? Yes, we **had.** / No, we **hadn't**.	• *When* I visited my mom last month, she had painted my old bedroom pink and (had) sold all my old books. • *By the time* he was 10, Johnny still hadn't learned to speak. • What had you achieved *by the time* you graduated from college? • I had *already* started my own business.

4 Connect the sentences using the past perfect tense, along with *just* or *already*. The first sentences have been completed for you.

1 I arrived at the airport at 7:30 p.m. The plane left at 7:29 p.m.

When I *arrived at the airport, the plane had just left.*

2 Jack read the book in 2002. He saw the movie in 2005.

Jack _____ before he

_____.

3 Lilly brushed her teeth at 9:45 p.m. Her mom offered her a snack at 9:46 p.m.

Lilly _____ when her mom

_____.

4 I got home at 8:00 p.m. My wife finished eating dinner at 7:15 p.m.

By the time I _____, my wife _____

_____.

5 Lisa went home at 10:00 p.m. We started serving coffee at 10:01 p.m.

Lisa _____

when we _____.

6 Tommy studied Chinese in 2010. He went to China in 2012.

Before Tommy _____,

he _____.

V. Now, Time to Speak!

5 Pair Work! Look at the timelines. With your partner, take turns describing the changes to the places over time. Use the model to help you.

Example

| Student A | By 1950, they'd put up a bookshelf, bought new chairs and . . . |
| Student B | By 1980, they'd installed a TV . . . |

1

| 1900 | 1950 | 1980 | 2010 |

get rid of (something unwanted) ➜ got rid of | repaint (the wall) ➜ repainted
install (a light / a TV) ➜ installed | replace (A with B) ➜ replaced

2

| February 2005 | March 2006 | January 2009 | September 2012 |

have (a baby) ➜ had | save (money) ➜ saved

3

| 7:00 a.m. | 9:00 a.m. | 12:00 p.m. | 3:00 p.m. |

set (the table) ➜ set | serve (guests) ➜ served

6 With your partner, take turns asking and answering the questions below.
You can use any of the three pictures given to help you answer.

| Student A | You looked so tired yesterday. How come? |
| Student B | I was tired because I hadn't eaten anything all day. |

1 You looked so tired yesterday. How come?

| run (a marathon) | eat | sleep |
| ➡ run | ➡ eaten | ➡ slept |

2 Why were you wearing an eye patch last Saturday?

| hit | go to (a party) | catch (a disease / an infection) |
| ➡ hit | ➡ been to | ➡ caught |

3 Why were you crying last night?

| break up (with your partner) | die | fire |
| ➡ broken up | ➡ died | ➡ fired |

4 Why did you scream so loudly earlier?

 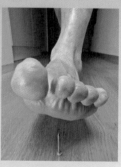 

| see (bugs) | step on (something sharp) | spill (tea / coffee) |
| ➡ seen | ➡ stepped | ➡ spilled |

7 With your partner, take turns reporting the events in the order suggested.

Pay attention to the actual order of events and where the narration begins.

Yesterday morning I woke up late because I'd forgotten to set my alarm clock the night before. And when I finally arrived at the train station, the train had already left.

Suggested reporting order: ❷ → ❶ → ❹ → ❸

| Because . . . the night before. | Yesterday morning I . . . | the train . . . | And when I finally . . . , |

A Suggested reporting order: ❸ → ❶ → ❷ → ❺ → ❹

— Kat . . . that morning, — and we . . . in the afternoon. — Yesterday evening I . . . — my favorite TV show . . . — When I . . . , though,

B Suggested reporting order: ❶ → ❷ → ❹ → ❸

— Last week I . . . , — but I . . . to put it in the fridge. — it . . . — So by the time . . . ,

Ⅵ. Now, Time to Pronounce!

> The auxiliary verb *had* is often shortened to **'d** when it comes after a subject pronoun. 助動詞 had 接在主格代名詞後面時，經常簡寫為 'd。

8 Listen and repeat the phrases that you hear.

(020)

I'd [aɪd] you'd [jud] he'd [hid] she'd [ʃid]

it'd [ˈɪtəd] we'd [wid] they'd [ðed]

9 Listen to the following sentences. Pay attention to whether the speaker uses the full form or the shortened form of the verb. Write (F) full or (S) short in the space provided.

(021)

| 1 _____ | 2 _____ | 3 _____ | 4 _____ | 5 _____ |
| 6 _____ | 7 _____ | 8 _____ | 9 _____ | 10 _____ |

UNIT 03

Talking About Life Changes and Memories
談論人生轉變與回憶

I. Topic Preview (022)

1 Talking about regular childhood activities 談論小時候的例行活動

When I was a kid, my family used to go skiing every winter.

What about in the summer?

In the summer, we would always go to the seaside.

That sounds great. I wish I had gone on trips with my family when I was younger.

2 Talking about how your life has changed since childhood 談論從小到現在的生活轉變

Have you always had a dog?

No, I used to have a cat when I was a kid.

Have you always been so slim?

No, I used to be overweight when I was a teenager.

3 Talking about changes in your habits 談論習慣的改變

You look very fit these days!

I used to sit in front of the TV all day, but now I work out five times a week.

4 Talking about changes in your preferences 談論喜好的改變

Do you like tennis?

I used to like tennis, but now I prefer soccer.

5 Describing how your life has changed since a certain event 描述人生如何因某個事件而轉變

How has your life changed since you got married?

John never used to come home late.

Well, I used to hang out a lot with my friends, but I don't anymore.

He comes home late all the time since he got that new job.

6 Recalling what you were like as a child 回憶自己小時候的情況

I used to believe in Santa when I was younger, and I used to have an imaginary friend.

II. Vocabulary & Phrases

get pocket money /
allowance
拿到零用錢

fight/argue with
one's brother/sister
和兄弟姊妹打架／吵架

make cookies
做餅乾

play Monopoly
玩大富翁

go stargazing
觀星

have/keep a pet
養寵物

be afraid of the dark
怕黑

be a troublemaker
調皮搗蛋

be a fussy eater
挑食

have an
imaginary friend
有虛構的朋友

graduate
畢業

take up a hobby
養成一項嗜好

join a club
加入社團

come back from
abroad
從國外回來

get promoted
升遷

Sentence Patterns

- When I was *a kid*, *my family* used to *play Monopoly* every *Christmas*.
- In the *evening*, *we* would always *go stargazing*.
- I wish I had *gone on trips with my family* when I was *younger*.
- Have you always *been so brave*?
  No, I used to *be afraid of the dark* when I was *little*.
- I used to *dye my hair pink*, but now I *dye it blue*.
- I used to like *white wine*, but now I prefer *red wine*.
- How has your life changed since you *got promoted*?
  I used to *worry about money*, but I don't anymore.
- Lisa never used to *read novels*. Since she *joined that book club*, she *reads a book* *every night*.

25

III. Now, Time to Listen!

1 Charlotte and Ben are talking about their childhoods. Check ☑ the topics they discuss.

(025)

a ○ b ○ c ○ d ○ e ○

➡ (026) Now listen again and circle the correct answers.

1 Ben used to go to the seaside / get pocket money every week / month.

2 Charlotte and her sister used to go stargazing / argue all the time.

3 Ben and his brother are / aren't good friends anymore.

4 Charlotte used to go abroad / go camping with her family every summer / winter.

5 Charlotte and her family would tell jokes / play Monopoly together.

6 Ben never / often went on family trips.

2 Listen to the following short conversations. Write the names of the people under their childhood picture.

(027)

Tina   Janet   Richard   Ellie   Mark

a   b   c   d   e

3 Listen to Oliver describe his friend Simon. How has Simon changed following the events in the table below? Look at the pictures and put them in the correct spots in the table. The first spot has been filled for you.

(028)

	1	2	3	4
then 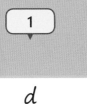	*d*			
event	 got married	got promoted	went to India for a vacation	 joined a dance class
now				

IV. Now, Grammar Time!

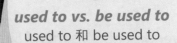

used to vs. be used to
used to 和 be used to

used to + verb used to + 動詞 用來描述過去的習慣、反覆進行的動作， 以及目前已經完成或改變的狀態	**be used to + noun** be used to + 名詞 用來談論你所熟悉、習慣的事物

• I used to *live* in London, but now I live in Beijing.
• He didn't use(d) to *read* a lot, but now he does.
• Did you use(d) to *go* on trips with your family?
  Yes, I **did**. / No I **didn't**.
• Where did they use(d) to *go* on vacations when they were kids?
• They used to *go* to Florida every year.
	• I've lived in Beijing for 10 years, so I am used to *eating* Chinese food.
	• He hasn't lived here long, so he is not used to *the accent*.
	• Are you used to *this kind of weather*?
	  Yes, I **am**. / No, I'm **not**.
	• What kind of hotel are you used to *staying* in?
	  I'm used to *staying* in five-star hotels.

In informal English, people often prefer to use "never used to" rather than "didn't use to."
英文口語通常使用「never used to」，而不使用「didn't use to」。

   I never used to like Chinese food, but I do now.

➔ *I didn't use(d) to like Chinese food, but I do now.*

4 Look at the pictures and choose "used to" or "be used to" to fill in the blanks.
The first sentence has been completed for you.

a

Sorry about my driving.
I _am not used to driving_
this new car yet. *(drive)*

b

I _____,
but I started because my wife
called me fat. *(exercise)*

c

My mom _____
_____ every
Christmas. *(make cookies)*

d

We _____
_____ named Lassie, but she
died when I was 10.
(have a dog)

e

Don't worry. He's fine.
He _____
_____, that's all. *(fly)*

f

A: How can you sleep?
   It's so noisy.
B: I _____.
   (the noise)

Would

We can often replace *used to* with *would* when talking about repeated past actions.
當我們談論反覆發生的過去事件時，通常會用 would 取代 used to。

My grandmother used to give me $10 for my birthday (every year).

→ My grandmother would give me $10 for my birthday (every year).

I used to go stargazing with my brother every time we went camping.

→ I would go stargazing with my brother every time we went camping.

BUT: You CAN NOT use "would" to talk about past states or habits.
但是：不能用 would 來談論過去的狀態或習慣。

x	I would smoke.		✓	I used to smoke.
x	I would have a dog.	→	✓	I used to have a dog.
x	I would like soccer.		✓	I used to like soccer.

❺ Complete the sentences using the words in the boxes. Some words will be used more than once.

use to · like · know · give · used to

play · own · would · have · read

1 I __used to__ _____ how to speak Italian, but I've forgotten it all now.

2 When I was a kid, my mother _____ _____ me $5 every week to buy candy.

3 I _____ _____ a beautiful red car, but I sold it five years ago.

4 I didn't _____ _____ classical music, but I really enjoy listening to it now.

5 Every year at Christmas, the whole family _____ _____ Monopoly together.

6 Did you _____ _____ an imaginary friend when you were a kid?

7 My father _____ _____ me a bedtime story every night when I was younger.

V. Now, Time to Speak!

6 Pair Work! Fill in the table below with as many differences between your childhood and the present day as you can. Then tell your partner about how you've changed.

 Note

If you want to talk about past ability with "used to," you need to use "be able to."
如果你要用「used to」來談論過去能力的時候，後面要接「be able to」。
*I used to **be able to** play piano, but I **can't** anymore.*

Example

childhood	now
Mom gave me pocket money every week.	I work.

Student A	My mom used to give me pocket money every week, but now I work.

childhood	now

7 With a partner take turns asking and answering the following questions. You can make some of the questions more relevant to your partner by replacing the words in **bold** with ideas of your own.

Examples

A	*Have you always been so **hardworking**?*
B	*No, when I was in high school, l I used to be lazy.*

A	*Have you always been so **hardworking**?*
B	*Yes, I've always been hardworking.*

Have you always been **a fussy eater**?	Have you always had **long hair**?
Have you always been afraid of **spiders**?	Have you always **bitten your nails**?
Have you always liked **rock music**?	Have you always **eaten so quickly**?

8 Group Work! Imagine you experienced a life-changing event. Decide how your life would have changed because of that event. Describe these changes to the class. Can they guess the event?

Example

A	*I never used to be able to speak French, but now I can.*
B	*Did you study abroad?*
A	*No. I used to visit my grandparents for the holidays, but now I go to Paris for the holidays.*
B	*Did you marry a Frenchman?*
A	*Yes, I did!*

Some life-changing events 一些人生大事

- ★ winning the lottery 中樂透
- ★ graduating from university 大學畢業
- ★ getting fired 被解雇
- ★ moving abroad 移居國外
- ★ having a baby 生小孩
- ★ being on TV 上電視

VI. Now, Time to Pronounce!

Sentence Stress 句子的重音 　　Part I

A word is stressed if it's said a little louder or for a little longer than other words.
如果我們將某一個字唸得比較大聲，或聲音拉得比較長，這個字就是被加了重音。

9 In an English sentence, the most important words are usually stressed.

 Listen to the following sentence and pay attention to the words that are stressed.

→ My <u>mo</u>ther used to **give** me <u>po</u>cket <u>mo</u>ney.

> The words "mother," "give," "pocket," and "money" are all stressed because they are most important to the meaning of the sentence.
>
> mother、give、pocket 和 money 都要加重音，因為它們是表達語意的重要詞彙。

 Listen and repeat the following sentences.

1 I <u>saw</u> a **great** <u>mo</u>vie on <u>Sat</u>urday.

2 Will you <u>come</u> with me to <u>see</u> the <u>doc</u>tor?

3 We used to **go** to Ja<u>pan</u> every <u>sum</u>mer for our va<u>ca</u>tion.

4 Can you <u>buy</u> me a <u>so</u>da when you <u>go</u> to the <u>store</u>?

> Look closely at the sentences above. Notice that the content words (verbs, nouns, adjectives, and adverbs) are all stressed, but the function words (**pronouns, prepositions, auxiliary verbs, etc.**) are not.
>
> 仔細看上面這幾個句子，注意到**內容詞**（即實詞，包含動詞、名詞、形容詞和副詞）都加了重音，而**功能詞**（即虛詞，包含代名詞、介系詞、助動詞等）則不加重音。

10 Before you listen to the following sentences, try to guess which words will be  stressed. Circle those words.

1 I play soccer with my brother every day after school.

2 He takes the train to work in the morning.

3 Have you eaten at this restaurant before?

4 My grandpa used to fall asleep in his chair.

5 Do you know how to get to the museum?

Chatting and Telling Personal Stories
閒聊與談論個人經歷

I. Topic Preview 032

1 *Joining a group conversation* 加入小組聊天

Hi guys, sorry to interrupt.

That's all right, Joe.

Hey, guys. What's going on?

So, what are we talking about?

Jim's telling us about his date last night.

We're just talking about the game last night.

2 *Reacting to what someone has said* 回應某人說的話

OK. So, we'd arranged to meet at seven . . .

But she turned up about an hour late . . .

Yeah, and then she ordered the most expensive thing on the menu.

Uh-huh.

No way!

Oh my God! Seriously?

3 *Continuing a conversation* 延續對話

OK, so what happened next?

Well, next we went for a walk.

Then what?

Well, then we kissed.

4 *Ending your turn and beginning someone else's*
結束自己的話，換對方發言

Anyway, it was really terrible.

I bet it was. Actually, the same thing happened to me two years ago . . .

II. Vocabulary & Phrases (033)

slam the door
甩門

Well . . .
change the subject
轉移話題

**suited to something/
someone**
適合某物／某人

throw up
嘔吐

be/get conned
被騙

gossip 八卦

foul 犯規

embarrassing
使人尷尬的

STOP
interrupt 打斷

weird 古怪的

Sentence Patterns (034)

Asking to join a conversation 要求加入對話
- Sorry to interrupt.
- Do you mind if I join you?
- You don't mind if I chat with you guys for a minute, do you?

Getting up to speed 趕上對話進度
- What are we talking about?
- What's happening?
- What's going on?
- What's the latest gossip?

Showing interest 表現出興趣
- Oh, really?
- Oh, yeah?
- Oh, right.

Showing you follow 表示有在聽
- Uh-huh.
- Mm-hm.

Continuing a conversation 延續對話
- And?
- Then what?
- What happened next?
- Then what happened?

Showing surprise/disbelief 表示驚訝／難以置信
- Oh, wow!
- No way!
- Oh my God!
- Seriously?
- Are you kidding?

Starting your turn 展開對話
- (I bet.) Actually . . .
- (I agree with you.) The thing is . . .
- (Wow.) Well . . .
- (Yeah. Right.) But . . .
- (Hmm. I don't know.) I think . . .

Ending your turn 結束自己的話題
- Anyway . . .
- So anyway . . .
- Yeah, so . . .
- So yeah . . .

III. Now, Time to Listen!

1 Listen to the conversation extracts. Match each one to the picture that best illustrates it.

(035)

 1

2

3

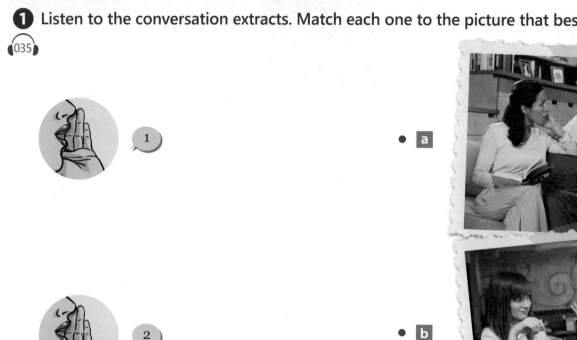

● a

● b

● c

(036) Listen again, and write down any key words or phrases that helped you make your decision.

1

sorry to interrupt

2

3

34

2 First, read the questions. Then listen to the following conversation between
Harry and Kate. Answer the questions by checking ☑ the correct box.

(037)

1 How does Harry end his turn?
- **a** ☐ Yeah, so it just . . .
- **b** ☐ So anyway, it just . . .

2 How does Kate begin her turn?
- **a** ☐ I bet. Actually, something . . .
- **b** ☐ Right. Well, something . . .

3 How does Harry express interest?
- **a** ☐ Oh, really?
- **b** ☐ Oh, yeah?

4 How does Harry show he follows?
- **a** ☐ Mm-hm.
- **b** ☐ Uh-huh.

5 How does Harry show surprise?
- **a** ☐ Oh my God! Seriously?
- **b** ☐ Are you kidding?

6 How does Kate end her turn?
- **a** ☐ So anyway, I know . . .
- **b** ☐ Yeah, so I know . . .

7 How does Harry begin his turn?
- **a** ☐ Right. Well, the thing is . . .
- **b** ☐ Yeah. So, the thing is . . .

3 Listen to the conversation and look at the chart below. Check ☑ who does what.

(038)

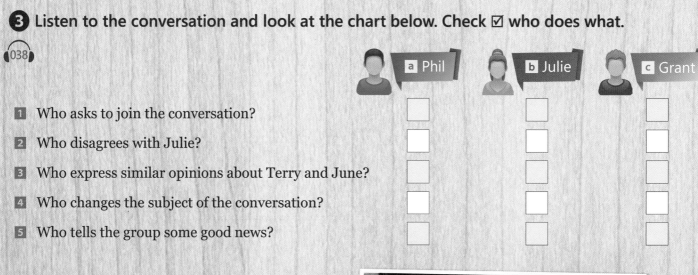

	a Phil	**b** Julie	**c** Grant
1 Who asks to join the conversation?	☐	☐	☐
2 Who disagrees with Julie?	☐	☐	☐
3 Who express similar opinions about Terry and June?	☐	☐	☐
4 Who changes the subject of the conversation?	☐	☐	☐
5 Who tells the group some good news?	☐	☐	☐

Transitional Expressions 轉折語
A transitional expression shows the connection between two ideas.
轉折語用來連接兩種不同的概念。

Sequence and addition 發生順序與補充說明	
• *then* 接著	We were winning, and then Simon fouled.
• *in addition* 除此之外	We lost. In addition to that, I hurt my leg.

Compare and contrast 比較和對比	
• *otherwise* 否則	I'm glad I quit; otherwise, I'd still be working for that terrible boss.
• *even so* 即便如此	I was tired, but even so, I still finished the project.

Show cause and effect 說明原因和結果	
• *so* 所以	We had a big argument, so we broke up.
• *as a result* 結果	I made the company a lot of money. As a result, I got promoted.

Give examples and conclusions 舉例和總結	
• *for example* 舉例來說	He's so lazy. For example, he never washes the dishes.
• *in short* 總之	I think she's rude; I think she's bad-tempered. In short, I don't like her.

❹ **Pair Work! Practice the dialogue below. Write a transitional expression in each blank.**

Yvonne	How did your meeting go, Jim?
Jim	Not so great; _____ I'd be buying everyone drinks right now.
Yvonne	Right. But _____, it can't have been that bad.
Jim	It was terrible. I arrived at the office late, and _____ to that, I forgot my laptop.
Yvonne	Oh my God! Seriously? _____, you couldn't give the presentation.
Jim	Exactly.
Yvonne	Oh man, that is bad. And _____, was your boss angry?
Jim	Of course. _____, he was furious. He shouted at me for hours, and _____ sent me home early. So yeah, pretty terrible.
Yvonne	Yeah. Well, I can see that now. But at least he didn't fire you. My boss, _____, fired someone for not wearing a tie!

V. Now, Time to Speak!

5 Listen to the conversation and practice it with your partner.

039

Will	**Hi, guys. Sorry to interrupt.**
Grace	That's OK. Come and join us.
Will	**Thanks. What's happening?**
Grace	I was just telling Jack about my date last week. It was so embarrassing.
Will	**Oh, really?**
Grace	Yeah. We went to that new French restaurant in town.
Will	**Mm-hm.**
Grace	And I ordered escargot by mistake.
Will	**Escargot? What's that?**
Grace	Snails!
Will	**No way! Are you kidding?**
Grace	Nope. So, I was eating them, and I started to feel really, really ill.
Will	**Uh-huh. Then what happened?**
Grace	Well, I threw up at the table.
Will	**Oh my God! Seriously?**
Grace	Yep. **Anyway**, it was the most embarrassing thing that's ever happened to me.
Will	**I bet. Actually**, something similar happened to me a few weeks ago.

Now use the stories below to create similar conversations.

One student should remember to ask to join the conversation, catch up, and show interest, surprise, and that he or she follows where necessary.

a Story: The Terrible Break up.

★ You broke up with your girlfriend/boyfriend last night.

★ You had a huge argument.

★ She threw your iPhone out the window.

b Gossip: Jerry Might Get Fired.

★ Jerry might get fired today.

★ Sandy heard him arguing with his boss.

★ Jerry insulted his boss.

★ He stormed out of the office.

c Good News: A New Job!

★ You went to the interview yesterday.

★ You had to take a test and answer lots of difficult questions.

★ The boss offered you the job there and then.

★ You were so surprised. You never thought you'd get the job.

VI. Now, Time to Pronounce!

Sentence Stress 句子的重音 | **Part II**

6 English has a natural rhythm. Try to keep the time between each stressed word the same. This way, the beats (stressed words) come at consistent intervals. To do this you might need to say some parts of the sentence faster or slower than others. *(040)*

We used to **go** to Ja**pan** every **su**mmer for our va**ca**tion.

time 1 = time 2 = time 3 = time 4

(041) **Practice:** Say the following key words along with the CD. Pay attention to the rhythm that's created. It might help to clap each time you say a stressed word.

Beat 1	Beat 2	Beat 3	Beat 4
go	**Japan**	**su**mmer	va**ca**tion

(042) Now listen again. Notice how the function words fit in between the beats. Try to say the sentence along with the CD. Again, clapping might help you keep to the rhythm.

	Beat 1		Beat 2		Beat 3		Beat 4
We used to	**go**	to	**Ja**pan	every	**su**mmer	for our	va**ca**tion.

7 Listen to the sentences and read along. (Circle) the beats. The first sentence has partly been done for you. *(043)*

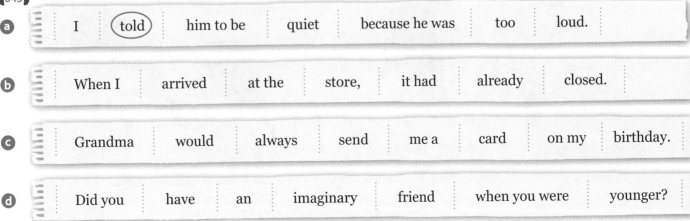

a I (told) him to be quiet because he was too loud.

b When I arrived at the store, it had already closed.

c Grandma would always send me a card on my birthday.

d Did you have an imaginary friend when you were younger?

Having an Argument 爭執

I. Topic Preview 044

1 Complaining and accusing 抱怨和指控

Why do you always interfere in my business?

You never listen to me!

It's so annoying when you talk down to me.

2 Defending yourself 自我辯護

You always make me clean the house. It's not fair.

Excuse me? When do you ever clean the house?

3 Contradicting someone 反駁他人

You're always so mean to me.

Are you kidding me? I'm never mean to you.

4 Passing the blame 推卸責任

It's not my fault.

Then whose fault is it?

Jerry made me do it.

Don't try to blame someone else.

5 Trying to end an argument 試圖結束爭吵

Just take it easy for a second.

You're so unreasonable!

II. Vocabulary & Phrases (045)

nag someone to do something
不斷叨唸別人去做事

interfere in someone's business
干涉別人的事

hog something
霸佔物品

talk down to someone
用言語貶損別人

talk behind someone's back
在背後說人壞話

blame someone
責怪別人

insult/mock someone
羞辱／嘲弄別人

take advantage of someone 利用別人

make noise
製造噪音

make a mess
搞得一團糟

cause trouble
惹麻煩

deny something
否認事情

(be) selfish
自私

(be) irresponsible
不負責任

cool off / calm down / take it easy
冷靜／鎮定／別著急

blow a fuse / lose your temper / flip out
勃然大怒／發脾氣／失控

Sentence Patterns (046)

Complaining and defending yourself 抱怨並為自己辯護

- You never _let me use the computer_.
  Are you kidding me? I always _let you use it_.
- Why do you always _have me babysit my brother_?
  When do _I_ ever _have you babysit your brother_?
- Why are you always _so selfish_?
  When am I ever _selfish_?
- I'm tired of _you talking down to me_.
  Since when do _I talk down to you_?

- You always _nag me to clean my room_.
  You're so wrong. I never _nag you_.
- It's so annoying when you _hog the TV like that_.
  Oh yeah? What about you?
- Why do you insist on _being so irresponsible_?
  How dare you _accuse me of being irresponsible_?

Passing the blame 推卸責任

- It's not my fault.
- It wasn't me. It was _John_.
- He/She made me do it.

Trying to end an argument 試著停止爭吵

- Calm down.
- Just _cool off_ for a second.
- Don't _blow a fuse_.

Now, Time to Listen!

1 **(047)** First, read the statements below. Then listen to James argue with his mother. Which statement is he responding to each time? Number the sentences from 1 to 6.

> **a** That's it. You're not going out with your friends this weekend. _____
>
> **b** Why do you insist on talking down to me like that? _____
>
> **c** I'm tired of you taking advantage of me and your father. _____
>
> **d** You never help around the house. You're so selfish. _____
>
> **e** You always cause trouble in this house. _____
>
> **f** You're irresponsible. You always make a mess. You never listen. You always . . . _____

2 **(048)** Now listen to the whole conversation and check your answers. Then fill in the blanks below.

1 _____? I always help around the house.

2 _____ you? You talk to me like I'm a child.

3 OK, OK. Don't _____.

4 That's _____. Why do you always _____ my business?

5 When do I ever _____ of you?

6 It's not _____. You always _____ to do things I don't want to do.

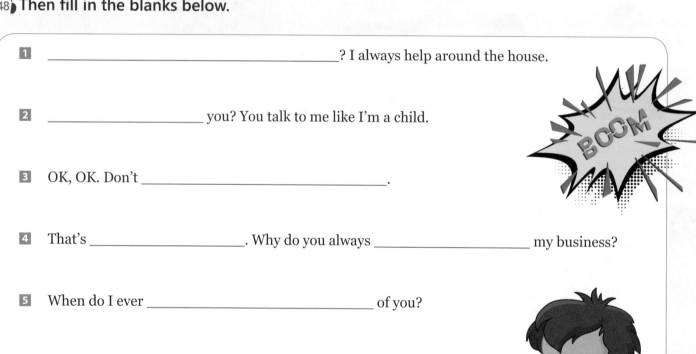

3 Listen to the argument between Jane and her colleague Max. Check ☑ the correct person's name to complete the sentence.

(049)

MAX	JANE		
☐	☐	**1**	never cleans up his/her things.
☐	☐	**2**	is accused of talking down to Jimmy.
☐	☐	**3**	walks away from the argument.
☐	☐	**4**	tries and fails to end the argument early.
☐	☐	**5**	accuses the other of talking behind people's backs.
☐	☐	**6**	is tired of the other person insulting his/her friends.
☐	☐	**7**	tries to blame someone else for his/her actions.

(050) Read the phrases below. Then listen to the argument again and check ☑ the phrases that Jane says.

☐ **a** It's so annoying when you don't clean up.

☐ **b** You never clean up your things.

☐ **c** How dare you speak to me like that?

☐ **d** Don't speak to me that way!

☐ **e** You're so wrong. I never cause trouble in the office!

☐ **f** Since when do I cause trouble?

☐ **g** I'm tired of you insulting my friends.

☐ **h** Why do you always insult my friends?

☐ **i** Fine. Whatever.

☐ **j** OK. You win.

IV. Now, Grammar Time!

Causative Verbs 使役動詞

let
to **allow** someone to do something 允許某人做某事

My mother will not **let** *me* **go** out with my friends.

have
to **order** someone to do something 命令某人做某事

The boss always **has** *John* **give** the presentation.

make
to **force** someone to do something 強迫某人做某事

I didn't want to, but he **made** *me* **steal** the money.

get
to **convince** someone to do something 說服某人做某事

I finally **got** *him* **to clean** up his mess.

4 Read the information below and make sentences with causative verbs. You may need to change the verb form.

Example

My mother won't allow me to go to the party.

→ My mother won't let me go to the party.

1 My father never orders me to wash the dishes.

→ My father never _____.

2 Why do you force me to work so hard?

→ Why do you _____?

3 When do I ever order you to tidy the office?

→ When do I ever _____?

4 You'll never convince me to do things your way.

→ You'll never _____.

5 Since when do I force you to stay home?

→ Since when do _____?

6 I'm tired of always forcing you to share the computer.

→ _____.

7 My grandma always allows me to do whatever I want at her house.

→ _____.

8 I don't know how to convince John to apologize to me.

→ _____.

9 Will you allow me to finish speaking, please?

→ _____?

10 It's so annoying when you order us to finish our reports over the weekend.

→ _____.

V. Now, Time to Speak!

5 Pair Work! With your partner, choose one of the groups below, and think of three things that they might argue about.

roommates

a married couple

classmates

colleagues

Example

Roommates: **1** making noise in the morning
2 making a mess in the kitchen
3 hogging the TV

(051) Now listen to the following dialogue and practice it with a partner.
Then have a similar conversation using the argument topics you just discussed.

Lydia	**Josh**, can you please stop **making so much noise so early in the morning**? It's driving me crazy.
Josh	What? Since when do I **make noise in the morning**?
Lydia	Uh, you **make noise** every **morning**. **You slam the fridge door; you stamp your feet**.
Josh	OK, OK. Well, what about you? You **always make a mess in the kitchen**.
Lydia	Are you kidding me? When do I ever **make a mess in the kitchen**?
Josh	All the time. **It's always dirty after you use it**. And I'm tired of you **hogging the TV, too**.
Lydia	You're so wrong. I never **hog the TV**. How dare you accuse me of **hogging the TV**?
Josh	All right, all right. Don't **flip out**. Just **calm down** for a second.
Lydia	Fine. Look, why don't we forget about this? We shouldn't argue.
Josh	I agree. I'm sorry.
Lydia	Me, too.

6 With a partner, discuss how to fill in the blanks in the following short dialogues. Share your ideas with the class, and then practice the dialogues.

1

Mom	Did you take some money from my purse, Jake?
Son	It wasn't me. _____.
Mom	I saw you do it. Don't try to _____
	_____.
Son	OK. It was me, but _____
	_____.

2

Eva	I'm tired of you always taking advantage of me!
Dan	Since when _____
	_____?
Eva	All the time. You _____
	_____.
Dan	OK, OK. Calm down. _____
	_____.

3

Daughter	Why do you always nag me to _____
	_____?
Dad	I have to because you're so _____.
Daughter	How dare _____
	_____?
Dad	Uh, you never _____;
	you never _____.

4

Ivy	_____
	talk behind my back, Peter.
Peter	What? _____
	_____.
Ivy	Don't _____. Jenny told me what you
	said. I'm tired of you _____.
Peter	It's not my fault. You _____
	_____.

VI Now, Time to Pronounce!

Tonic Stress 語調重音

7 Listen and repeat the following sentence.

(052)

> Why **are** you **al**ways so **sel**fish?

The words "why," "always," and "selfish" are all stressed. However, the last word, "selfish," receives extra stress. This extra stress is called the "tonic stress," and it usually comes on the last stressed word in a sentence.

why、always 和 selfish 都是重音字，但是最後一個 selfish 的發音要特別加重，我們稱之為「語調重音」，通常會落在句子的最後一個重音字。

(053) ➤ Listen and repeat the following sentences. Pay attention to the tonic stress.

- ★ I **ne**ver **cause trou**ble in the **of**fice.
- ★ **Why** do you in**sist** on **be**ing so irre**spon**sible?
- ★ **Stop** inter**fe**ring in my **bus**iness!
- ★ **Don't try** to **blame some**one **else**.
- ★ **When** do I **ev**er in**sult you**?

8 BUT we can change the position of the tonic stress in order to emphasize certain words or express a contrast. When we do this, the stress can fall on any word you want to emphasize (e.g., a function word). It doesn't have to fall on a content word.

(054) ➤ Listen again to the sentences. Circle the word that is given the tonic stress.

1 Why are you always so selfish?

2 I never cause trouble in the office.

3 Why do you insist on being so irresponsible?

4 Stop interfering in my business!

5 Don't try to blame someone else.

6 When do I ever insult you?

> Discuss with the class where else the tonic stress could occur in these sentences. How would the meaning change if the position of the tonic stress were different?

Talking About Regrets 談論遺憾

I. Topic Preview (055)

1 Talking about bad decisions 談論錯誤的決定

I wish I hadn't quit my job. It was a really bad decision.

You could have been promoted by now.

2 Talking about regrettable past states 談論過去令人遺憾的情形

Do you have any regrets?

I could have studied harder in school, I guess.

3 Talking about regrettable past behavior 談論過去令人遺憾的行為

What's your biggest regret?

I shouldn't have been so mean to my mom when I was a teenager.

4 Things you should have done but didn't 過去該做而未做的事

It's a pity you can't speak Spanish, isn't it?

HABLA ESPAÑOL?

I should have paid more attention in Spanish class.

5 How things could have been different 情勢可能如何轉變

If you had prepared for the interview, would it have made a difference?

Yes, if I had prepared for the interview, I think I would have got that job.

How would your life be different now if you'd married Yumi instead of marrying Claire?

Claire

Yumi

Well, I would probably be happier, and I'd be living in Japan instead of England.

II. Vocabulary & Phrases 〔056〕

quit one's job
辭職

work harder
更努力工作

ask someone out
追求某人

pay more attention
更加專注

turn someone down
拒絕某人

leave home
離家

remember/forget something
記得／忘記某事

fall out with someone
和某人爭吵

make up with someone
和某人和好

keep in touch with someone
和某人保持聯絡

drop out of school
輟學／退學

travel more
提高旅行次數

give up something
放棄某事

be nice
善良

be cruel
殘暴

be more thoughtful
更貼心

finish something
完成某事

Sentence Patterns 〔057〕

- Do you have any regrets?
  What's your biggest regret?
- I wish I had/hadn't *given up learning the piano*.
- I could have *studied harder at school*.
- I should/shouldn't have *left home when I was 16*.
- It's a pity you *don't talk to Pete anymore*, isn't it?
- I should have *kept in touch with him*.

- If you had *studied history*, would it have made a difference?
  How would your life be different now if you had *studied business* (instead of *dropping out of school*)?
  What if you had *studied math*?
- If I had *studied business*, I would have *become a businessman*.
- I would *be a teacher* now (instead of *being unemployed*).
- I could have *made a million dollars* by now.

49

1 Listen to the following dialogue. Check ☑ the things that Sally did. Then circle the R if Sally regrets doing it.

058

a	b Spain	c
☐ R	☐ R	☐ R

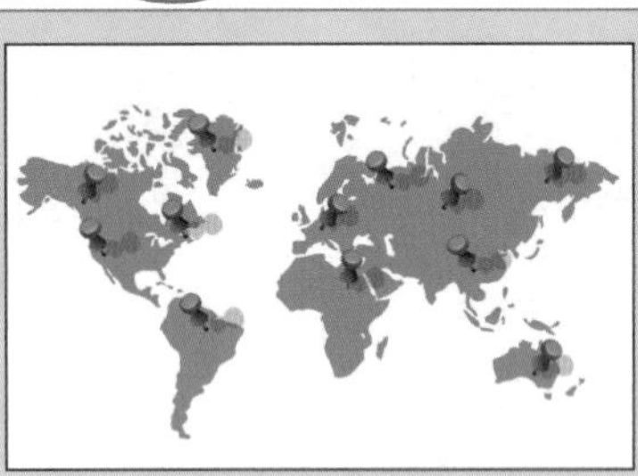

d	e	f
☐ R	☐ R	☐ R

059 Listen again and fill in the blanks with the expressions that Sally and the man use.

1 If I'd _____ more, I _____ so many countries by now.

2 Do you think _____ good friends now _____?

3 I could _____, I guess.

4 I _____ Chris Martin when he asked me out.

2 Listen to Joey's conversations. Check ☑ what Joey regrets in each one.

060

Joey regrets _____.

1
- a ☐ breaking up with his girlfriend
- b ☐ not being thoughtful enough
- c ☐ being too nice

2
- a ☐ not traveling to France more often
- b ☐ learning French in school
- c ☐ not paying attention in French class

3
- a ☐ giving up learning the piano
- b ☐ never learning the piano
- c ☐ spending too much time learning the piano

	a ☐	not keeping in touch with Pete
4	b ☐	being friends with Pete
	c ☐	forgetting Pete's birthday

	a ☐	talking to his landlady
5	b ☐	quitting his job
	c ☐	renting that apartment

❸ First, look at the answers to the following questions. Then listen to Mel, Simon, and
Daisy talk about their time at college and take notes. Who do you think the answers
belong to? Write the person's name in the space given.

061

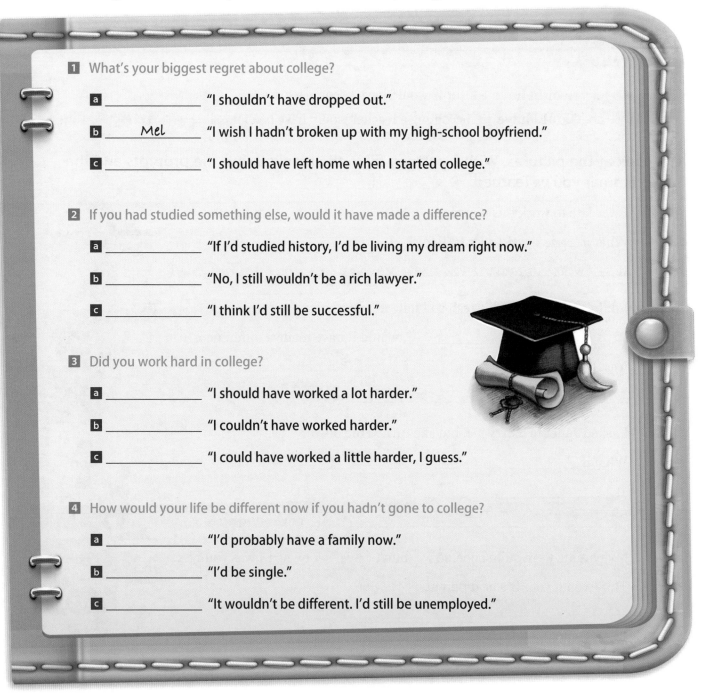

1 What's your biggest regret about college?

    a _____ "I shouldn't have dropped out."

    b _____Mel_____ "I wish I hadn't broken up with my high-school boyfriend."

    c _____ "I should have left home when I started college."

2 If you had studied something else, would it have made a difference?

    a _____ "If I'd studied history, I'd be living my dream right now."

    b _____ "No, I still wouldn't be a rich lawyer."

    c _____ "I think I'd still be successful."

3 Did you work hard in college?

    a _____ "I should have worked a lot harder."

    b _____ "I couldn't have worked harder."

    c _____ "I could have worked a little harder, I guess."

4 How would your life be different now if you hadn't gone to college?

    a _____ "I'd probably have a family now."

    b _____ "I'd be single."

    c _____ "It wouldn't be different. I'd still be unemployed."

IV. Now, Grammar Time!

Things that happened 已發生的事	I studied law, so I became a lawyer. OR I studied law, so I am a lawyer now.

the past   now

I studied law.   I became a lawyer.   I am a lawyer.

If I had studied history . . .   I would/could have become a teacher.   I would be a teacher.

Things that didn't happen 未發生的事	BUT If I had studied history, I could/would have become a teacher (by now). OR If I had studied history, I could/would be a teacher (now). ★ 記得在 had 和 have 之後要接**過去分詞**。

Note

"**would have**" → 100% would have become a teacher 一定會成為老師

"**could have**" → becoming a teacher would have been possible 可能會成為老師

❹ **Look at the pictures. With a partner, fill in the blanks using the prompts and the grammar you've learned.**

1 A   I was late to work this morning.

    B   What if _you'd woken up earlier_ ?

    A   If _I'd woken up earlier, I would have been on time_ . *(be on time)*

2 A   I didn't study for the big test, so I failed.

    B   If _____, would it have made a difference?

    A   Yes. If _____,

             _____. *(pass)*

3 A   I asked Janet to marry me, but she turned me down.

    B   What if _____?

    A   If _____,

             _____ now. *(engage)*

4 A   My parents were quite poor, so we didn't travel a lot when I was younger.

    B   How would your life be different

        if _____?

    A   If _____, _____

             _____ by now. *(visit more countries)*

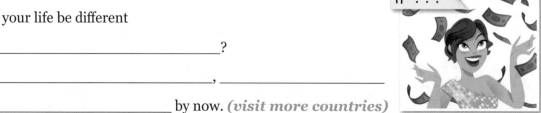

IF . . .

IF . . .

IF . . .

IF . . .

V. Now, Time to Speak!

5 Pair Work! Listen to the following conversation and then practice it with a partner.
Replace the phrases in color with ones from the word bank.

(062)

WORD BANK

- 💔 asked out Hannah
- 💔 thrown away that lottery ticket
- 💔 gone to that party
- 💔 crashed my car
- 💔 bought that diamond necklace

- 💔 bought a private island
- 💔 saved face
- 💔 kept my job
- 💔 saved a lot of money
- 💔 played in the big game

- 💔 lost a million dollars
- 💔 wasted all my money
- 💔 got turned down
- 💔 kissed my boss
- 💔 broken my leg

- 💔 been more careful
- 💔 stayed at home
- 💔 been less greedy
- 💔 listened to your advice
- 💔 driven more slowly

Kristen : What's your biggest regret, Robert?

Robert : Well, I wish I hadn't cheated on that test and
got thrown out of school.

Kristen : Yeah, that was a pity.

Robert : I know. If I hadn't cheated, I could have become a doctor.
How about you? Do you have any regrets?

Kristen : Yeah. I shouldn't have stolen that watch.
I could have been more honest, I guess.

Robert : And if you hadn't stolen that watch?

Kristen : I wouldn't have spent two years in jail.

6 Group Work! Ask your classmates if they have any regrets. Write down their regrets and ask a follow-up question. Write this extra information in the Comment column.

Example

Student A	What's your biggest regret, Linda? / Do you have any regrets, Linda?
Linda	Umm . . . I wish I had kept in touch with my friend Sarah from elementary school.
Student A	Why didn't you keep in touch with her?
Linda	Because I lost her phone number.

Name	Regret	Comment
Linda	I wish I had kept in touch with my friend Sarah from elementary school.	lost her phone number

Name	Regret	Comment

➡ Now share your findings with the class.

Example

| Student A | Linda wishes she had kept in touch with her friend from elementary school. She didn't keep in touch because she lost her phone number. |

VI. Now, Time to Pronounce!

Linking Sounds 連音

Being able to link sounds in English will make you sound more fluent. Here are some tips to help you link certain sounds. 使用連音能讓英文聽起來更流利，下列是朗讀某些連音的小技巧。

Q▾ Linking two vowel sounds

When a word that begins with a vowel sound follows a word that ends with a vowel sound (e.g. go over, we are, try again), we add an extra sound between the two words. This sound is either [w] or [j]. 當一個以母音開頭的單字，接在一個以母音結尾的單字後面時（例如：go over、we are、try again），我們會在兩個字中間插入 [w] 或 [j] 的音。

7 Listen and repeat the following phrases.

| • he is [hijɪz] | • enjoy it [ɪnˈdʒɔijɪt] | • day after [deˈjæftɚ] |
| • know it [nowɪt] | • now on [naʊwɔn] | • show us [ʃowʌs] |

➡️ (064) Listen to the CD. Do you hear a [w] or a [j] sound linking the words? (Circle) the sound that you hear.

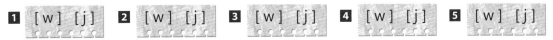

1 [w] [j]　**2** [w] [j]　**3** [w] [j]　**4** [w] [j]　**5** [w] [j]

8 When [t] or [d] comes before [j] (e.g., would you, can't you), we can join the (065) two separate sounds into one new sound.

• [t] + [j] = [tʃ]　　• [d] + [j] = [dʒ]

➡️ (066) Listen and repeat the following phrases. First they are pronounced separately and then with the new, joined sound.

won't you	[wont ju]	[wontʃu]	could you	[kʊd ju]	[kʊdʒu]
put your	[pʊt jʊr]	[pʊtʃʊr]	should you	[ʃʊd ju]	[ʃʊdʒu]
meet you	[mit ju]	[mitʃu]	did you	[dɪd ju]	[dɪdʒu]

➡️ (067) Listen to the CD. Do you hear the words spoken separately or linked together? Fill in the blanks with the correct phonetic symbols.

1 [wʊ d̲ j̲ u]　**2** [ʃʊdən_____u]　**3** [dɪ_____u]　**4** [don_____u]

5 [kʊdən_____u]　**6** [mi_____u]　**7** [kʊ_____u]　**8** [pʊ_____ʊɚ]

🔍▾ **Omitting [t] and [d]**

When a [t] or [d] sound comes at the end of a word, it can sometimes be dropped altogether.
字尾 [t] 和 [d] 的發音有時可以省略。

9 Listen and repeat the following phrases.
(068) First they are pronounced separately and then with the dropped [t] or [d].

first date	[fɝst det]	[fɝsdet]	and then	[ənd ðɛn]	[ənðɛn]
went in	[wɛnt ɪn]	[wɛnɪn]	second-hand	[ˈsɛkənd hænd]	[ˈsɛkənhænd]
best friend	[bɛst frɛnd]	[bɛsfrɛnd]	sand castle	[sænd ˈkæsl̩]	[sænˈkæsl̩]

➡️ (069) Listen and practice saying the following sentences, dropping the [t] or [d] sound where indicated.

★ Last night I went on a first date with a short man.

★ The blond girl smiled and said, "You sound nice."

Relationships
人際關係

I. Topic Preview 070

1 Talking about the qualities of a good friend 談論作為好朋友的特質

Good friends should always support each other.

I think so, too. And they shouldn't talk behind each other's backs, either.

2 Talking about your circle of friends 談論你的朋友圈

 Who's your best friend?

 Jessie is my best friend.

 How long have you known her?

 About 10 years.

 So is she your oldest friend, too?

 Yes, that's right!

Jessie

Darren

How well do you know Darren?

Not very well. He's just an acquaintance. Are you two good friends?

Yes, but we haven't known each other very long.

3 Talking about compatibility 談論是否合得來

I like dancing, and so does he. We're such a good match.

I like dogs, but he likes cats. I don't think we're compatible.

4 Talking about what relationships need 談論維持良好關係的秘訣

What do you think makes a good relationship?

I think a good relationship needs trust and patience.

II. Vocabulary & Phrases 🎧 071

share secrets with each
other / keep secrets
from each other
分享秘密／保守秘密

support each other
互相支持

have similar/
different
interests
擁有類似／
不同的興趣

enjoy each
other's company
享受彼此的陪伴

irritate each
other
激怒對方

make each other
laugh 逗對方笑

upset each other
惹對方生氣

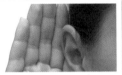

listen to each
other's problems /
ignore each other
聆聽彼此的心事／
忽略對方

care about each other
互相關心

best friend
最好的朋友

acquaintance
熟人

honesty /
be honest
誠實／做人誠實

patience /
be patient
耐心／有耐心

understanding /
be understanding
理解／善解人意

affection /
be affectionate
情感／深情的

trust
信任

respect
尊敬

Sentence Patterns 🎧 072

- Good friends should _always_ _support each other_.
- Who's your _oldest_ friend?
  Mark is my _oldest_ friend.
- How long have you known him/her?
  I've known him/her for about _seven years_. /
  I've known him/her since _high school_.
- How did you meet?
  We met _at work_.
- How well do you know _Jenny_?
  Not very well. She is just a _colleague_. /
  Very well. She is my _roommate_.
- I like _classical music_, and so does he/she.

- We're such a good match. /
  We're on the same wavelength.
- Are you two _best_ friends?
  Yes, but we haven't known each other very long. /
  Yes. We've known each other for _10_ years. /
  No, we're just _acquaintances_.
- I like _going out_, but he likes _staying in_.
  I don't think we're compatible.
- What do you think makes a good _relationship_?
  I think a good _relationship_ needs _honesty_ and
  affection. /
  You need to _be honest_ and _understanding_.

1 Mark and Lisa are at a party. Listen to their conversation and complete the table about Mark's friends.

(073)

Mark's Friends

	Jane	Sam	Ollie	Tanya
Relationship				girlfriend
Where they met	junior high school			
How long they've known each other		three years		

2 Listen to Jan and Billy talk about friendship. Then, decide whether the following statements are true (T) or false (F). Correct the mistakes in the false statements.

(074)

1 ____F____ Jack is Billy's ~~oldest~~ friend.
                                  best

2 _____ Billy thinks good friends should always listen to each other's problems.

3 _____ Billy and Jack have similar interests.

4 _____ Billy and Jack like soccer and rock music.

5 _____ Billy and Jack share secrets with each other.

6 _____ Billy thinks a good friendship needs affection.

7 _____ Jan thinks you shouldn't keep secrets from your friends.

8 _____ Jan thinks a good friendship needs patience.

58

3 Listen to Ashley talking about his relationship with Josie. Check ☑ the things that
Ashley thinks you need to have or to do to make a good relationship.

(075)

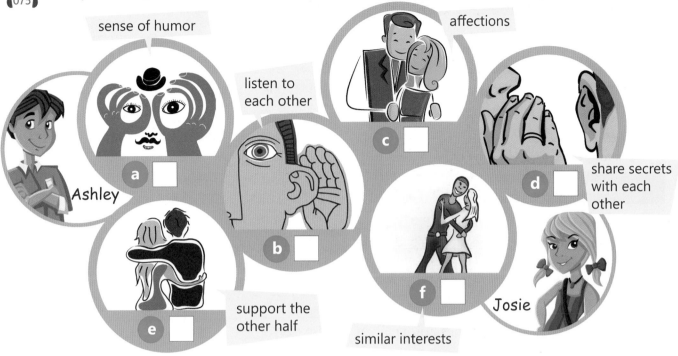

sense of humor

affections

listen to
each other

share secrets
with each
other

Ashley

a ☐

c ☐

d ☐

b ☐

f ☐

e ☐

support the
other half

Josie

similar interests

(076) Listen again and fill in the blanks with the expressions that Ashley says.

1 A good relationship _____.

2 You should _____ each other.

3 _____ is really important for a relationship.

4 _____ have similar interests, _____.

5 Josie and I aren't _____.

6 Josie doesn't _____ me, either.

7 I just don't think we're very _____.

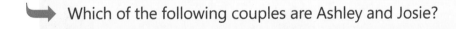

Which of the following couples are Ashley and Josie?

a ☐

b ☐

c ☐

IV. Now, Grammar Time!

too, also, so, either, neither
These words add agreeing information to an original statement.
這些單字的句子，與原始句持一致的立場。

Affirmative + Affirmative 肯定句 + 肯定句	**Affirmative + Negative** 肯定句 + 否定句
• I like baseball. <u>So *does* Jerry.</u> • You should trust each other. <u>You *should also* support each other.</u> • He is my best friend. <u>He *is* my oldest friend, too.</u>	• *She hates baseball.* <u>She *doesn't like* basketball, either.</u> • *A good relationship needs trust.* <u>You also *shouldn't* lie to each other.</u>
Negative + Affirmative 否定句 + 肯定句	**Negative + Negative** 否定句 + 否定句
• Katie *doesn't* support me. <u>She *lies* to me, too.</u> • He *isn't* a good boyfriend. <u>He *is* also a bad friend.</u>	• He *isn't* my friend. <u>Neither *are* you.</u> (neither = not either) • We *don't respect* each other. <u>We *don't trust* each other, either.</u>

"Also" usually comes **before a verb** 「also」通常用於動詞之前
→ He **also** *likes* horror movies.
BUT "also" comes **after the verb "be."** 但是「also」要用於 be 動詞之後
→ He *is* **also** my oldest friend.

❹ **Read what Tom, Richard, and Harry say. Then make sentences with "so" and "neither."**

TOM
• I'm not keen on Italian food.
• I think good friends should make each other laugh.
• I love to drive fast cars.
• I don't think Harry is very funny.
• I don't trust Richard.
• I've known Richard for a year.

RICHARD
• I like action movies.
• I think good friends should make each other laugh.
• I don't like soccer.
• I love to drive fast cars.
• I'm Tom's roommate.
• I don't think Harry is very funny.

HARRY
• I'm not keen on Italian food.
• I like action movies.
• I don't like soccer.
• I'm Tom's roommate.
• I don't trust Richard.
• I've known Richard for a year.

60

5 Fill in the blanks in the following sentences with the words provided.
You will need to use some of the words more than once.

should	shouldn't	either
has	doesn't	is
also	have	too

1. You should support each other, and you _____ listen to each other's problems,

   _____.

2. A good relationship needs trust, and it _____ good to make each other laugh.

3. Katie isn't mean, and she _____ a lot of patience, _____.

4. Sam and I don't make each other laugh, and we _____ different interests.

5. She doesn't care about you, and she _____ care about me, _____.

6. Good friends should enjoy each other's company, and they _____ argue.

   ➡ Now use *either*, *also*, and *too* to connect these sentences.

Examples

Student A	She is a bad friend, and she isn't a good roommate, **either**.
Student B	She isn't a good roommate, and she is **also** a bad friend.

1. She isn't a good roommate. She is a bad friend.

   _____

2. Friends should be affectionate with each other. Friends shouldn't upset each other.

   _____

3. We don't make each other laugh. We irritate each other all the time.

   _____

4. We are on the same wavelength. We don't keep secrets from each other.

   _____

5. He ignores me. He doesn't respect me.

   _____

V. Now, Time to Speak!

6 Pair Work! Tell your partner about your best friend. Use the following questions to help you.

> ★ Is he/she your oldest friend, too?
>
> ★ How long have you known each other?
>
> ★ How/Where did you meet?
>
> ★ What similar interests do you have?
>
> ★ Why are you such good friends?

7 Group Work! Brainstorm different kinds of relationships. Choose one and discuss what you think that relationship needs to be successful.

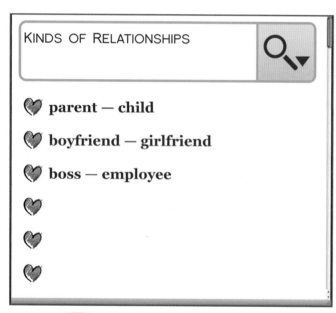

KINDS OF RELATIONSHIPS
🖤 parent — child
🖤 boyfriend — girlfriend
🖤 boss — employee
🖤
🖤
🖤

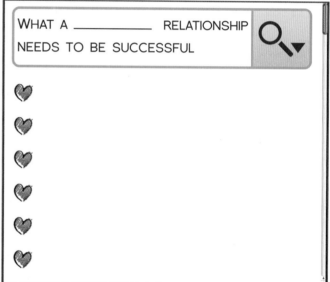

WHAT A _____ RELATIONSHIP NEEDS TO BE SUCCESSFUL

Example

Student A	A good parent-child relationship needs respect and love.
Student B	Yes. You also need to be honest with each other.
Student A	Parents should trust their children. And children should listen to their parents, too.

8 Have you ever heard the phrase "Blood is thicker than water"? What do you think it means? Do you agree with the phrase? Why or why not?

VI. Now, Time to Pronounce!

Contrastive Stress

Contrastive stress is when you move the tonic stress from its usual position at the end of a sentence to a word that you want to emphasize as a contrast or correction.
把語調的重音從平常句尾的位置，移到你想強調的單字上，作為對比或修正時，即稱為對比重音。

9 (077) Use contrastive stress to correct a mistake. Move the tonic stress to the word you wish to correct.

> Read the following statement. Then listen to and repeat the correcting statements.

"Jack went to Australia last summer on vacation."

→ No! **Sarah** went to Australia last summer on vacation, not Jack.

→ No! Jack went to Australia last summer on **business**, not on vacation.

(078) Listen to the following sentences correct a statement. Listen to the stress, and check ☑ the correct ending to the sentence.

1	ⓐ ☐ . . . not Alice. ⓑ ☐ . . . not my oldest.	**2**	ⓐ ☐ . . . not Jessie. ⓑ ☐ . . . not at school.
3	ⓐ ☐ . . . not a little. ⓑ ☐ . . . not patient.	**4**	ⓐ ☐ . . . not affection. ⓑ ☐ . . . not a friendship.
5	ⓐ ☐ . . . not 10. ⓑ ☐ . . . not months.	**6**	ⓐ ☐ . . . not you. ⓑ ☐ . . . not hates me.

10 You can also use contrastive stress to contrast two different things.

Move the tonic stress to the word you wish to contrast.

(079) Listen to the following statement. Then listen to and repeat the contrasting statements.

"I met your friend John at Jane's birthday party."

→ Oh, I met your friend **Carol** at the party.

→ Oh, I met John at Jane's **Christmas** party.

(080) Read the sentences and then listen to the contrast.
Check ☑ the sentence that is being contrasted.

1	ⓐ ☐ Simon is a really nice roommate. ⓑ ☐ John is a really nice boss.	**2**	ⓐ ☐ I've known Peter for five years. ⓑ ☐ I've known Sally for three years.
3	ⓐ ☐ I think a good friendship needs honesty. ⓑ ☐ I think a good marriage needs respect.	**4**	ⓐ ☐ Jane isn't very understanding. ⓑ ☐ Jack isn't very patient.
5	ⓐ ☐ A good boyfriend should support you. ⓑ ☐ A good friend should care about you.	**6**	ⓐ ☐ I met Eric in a nightclub. ⓑ ☐ I met James at work.

I. Topic Preview

 081

1 Talking about your income 談論收入

How much do you make each month?

I make $2,000 a month at my job.

Do you have any extra income?

I make an extra $200 a month selling stuff on eBay.

2 Talking about your outgoings 談論支出

How much do you spend on essentials every month?

I spend $1,000 on rent, $300 on utility bills, and $150 on groceries.

How much do you spend on luxury items?

I spend about $300 on new clothes and maybe $150 on books and DVDs.

3 Talking about saving money 談論儲蓄

 So you're saving about $200 a month.

That's not enough. I should be saving more than that.

How much do you want to be saving?

I want to be saving at least $500 a month.

4 Talking about balancing your spending 談論平衡消費

You spend so much on clothes that you don't have enough money to buy groceries!

I promise that I'll spend less money on clothes this month.

 How much are you going to budget for groceries this month?

I'm going to budget $200 for groceries, and $100 for new clothes.

II. Vocabulary & Phrases (082)

tutor 當家教

sell things online
上網賣東西

recycle
資源回收

write a blog 寫部落格

babysit 當保母

essentials 必需品
other expenses 其他支出
luxury items 奢侈品
entertainment 娛樂

groceries
日常用品

phone/Internet bill
電話費／網路費

cable bill
有線電視費

utility bill
水電費

health insurance
健康保險

eating out
外食

gym membership
加入健身房

classes
課程

**transportation
(gas / train tickets)**
交通費（汽油／火車票）

Sentence Patterns (083)

- How much do you make each month?
  I make _$2,000_ a month at my job.
- Do you have any extra income?
  I make an extra _$200_ a month _tutoring_.
- Maybe you could _babysit_ in your spare time to make some extra money.
- How much do you spend on _essentials_ every month?
  I spend _$1,000_ on _rent_, _$200_ on _utility bills_, and _$150_ on _groceries_.
- What other expenses do you have?
  There's _my health insurance_. That's _$20_ a month.

- How much do you want to be saving?
  I want to be saving at least _$500_ a month. /
  I should be saving _$300_ a month.
- You're really overspending!
  You need to cut back on _transportation_.
- You spend so much on your _gym membership_ that you don't have enough money to _pay your utility bills_!
- I promise that I'll spend less money on _going out_ this month.
- How much are you going to budget for _eating out_ this month?
  I'm going to budget _$250_ for _eating out_.

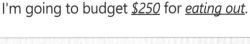

Now, Time to Listen!

1 Danny and Linda are discussing Danny's financial situation. Listen to their conversation and answer the following questions.

(084)

1 What's Danny's monthly salary?

a ☐ $2,200

b ☐ $2,500

c ☐ $3,000

2 Does Danny make any extra income?

a ☐ Yes

→ If "Yes," how much? $_____.

b ☐ No

3 On which of the following does Danny spend the most money?

a ☐ Eating out

b ☐ Going clubbing

c ☐ Spanish class

4 Which of the following does Danny not spend any money on?

a ☐ Rent

b ☐ Groceries

c ☐ Transportation

2 Listen again and fill in Danny's ledger.

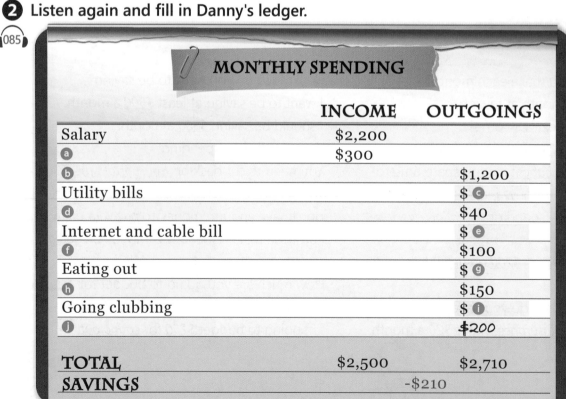

MONTHLY SPENDING

	INCOME	OUTGOINGS
Salary	$2,200	
a	$300	
b		$1,200
Utility bills		$ **c**
d		$40
Internet and cable bill		$ **e**
f		$100
Eating out		$ **g**
h		$150
Going clubbing		$ **i**
j		$200
TOTAL	$2,500	$2,710
SAVINGS		-$210

66

3 Listen to the second half of Danny and Linda's conversation. Check ☑ the changes that Linda suggests.

🎧 086

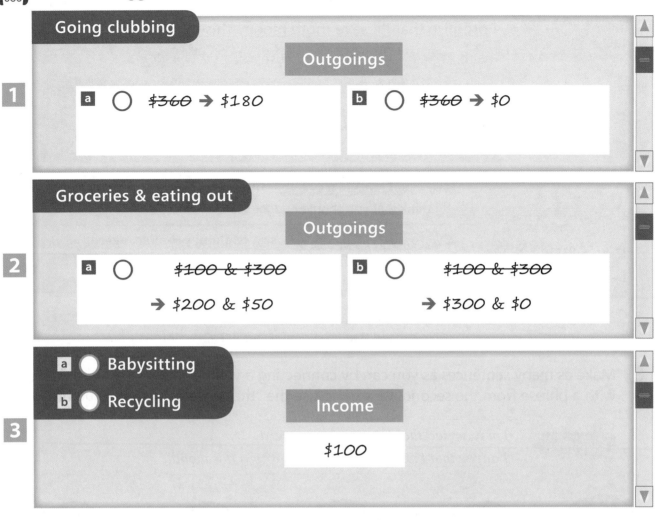

Going clubbing

Outgoings

1 a ○ $360 → $180   b ○ $360 → $0

Groceries & eating out

Outgoings

2 a ○ $100 & $300 → $200 & $50   b ○ $100 & $300 → $300 & $0

3 a ○ Babysitting
   b ○ Recycling

Income

$100

🎧 087 ➡ Listen again and fill in the blanks with the expressions that Linda and Danny say.

1 Wow! You're really _____.

2 I know. I'm _____ so much _____ clubbing that I can't

_____.

3 Right. And you need to _____ eating out.

4 Good idea. So how much should I _____?

5 So then I'd actually be saving $_____ a month. I _____

more than that, though.

6 Maybe you could _____ in your _____ for some extra

money.

that + noun clause
that + 名詞子句

I <u>promise</u> that <u>I'll save more money this month</u>.

verb 動詞　　　object (noun clause) 受詞（名詞子句）

The clause "I'll save more money this month" is a clause that acts as a noun. Here it's the object of the verb "promise."
「I'll save more money this month」是作名詞用的子句，在這裡作動詞「promise」的受詞。

We often use "that + noun clause" after . . .
這些詞彙後面通常接「that + 名詞子句」

1 verbs of thinking 思考動詞　**think, believe, know, understand . . .**
I **think** <u>that</u> you should budget $100 for luxury items.

2 verbs of saying 說話動詞　**say, explain, promise, agree . . .**
I **agree** <u>that</u> I overspend.
She **explained** <u>that</u> I spend too much on eating out.

3 adjectives of feeling 感覺形容詞　**happy, sad, excited, angry . . .**
I'm **excited** <u>that</u> I can now save $300 a month!

❹ Make as many sentences as you can by connecting a verb/adjective from the first box with a phrase from the second. Be sure to use the "that + noun clause" structure.

Examples

*I'm **worried** that I can't **pay the rent**.*
*I **agree** that I need to **spend less money** this month.*

| worried 擔心的 | disappointed 失望的 | agree 同意 | promise 承諾 | understand 了解 |

| pay the rent 付租金 | go clubbing 去夜總會 | spend less money 少花錢 | earn some extra money 賺外快 | cut back on eating out 減少外食 |

V. Now, Time to Speak!

5 Pair Work! With your partner, discuss how to fill in the blanks in the following short dialogues. Share your ideas with the class, and then practice the dialogues.

Ⓐ

A   How much do you spend on essentials each month?

B   I spend $1,500 on _____ and $200 on _____.

A   OK. What other expenses _____?

B   Well, there's health insurance, gym membership, and _____.

A   Do you spend a lot of money on _____?

B   Yes, quite a lot. I spend about $300 a month on _____ and _____.

A   And _____?

B   I save $500 a month, but I should _____.

Ⓑ

A   Oh, no! I don't think I can pay _____ this month!

B   That's because _____.

A   What can I do?

B   Maybe you could _____.

A   OK, but what about next month?

B   You should _____.

6 With your partner, ask and answer the following questions.

1 What's your main source of income?

My main source of income is _____.

2 Do you make any extra income?

Yes/No, _____.

3 How much do you spend on essentials / luxury items / entertainment each month?

I spend $_____ on _____.

4 Excluding rent and utility bills, what do you spend the most on each month? Do you think it's worth it?

I spend the most on _____. I think _____.

5 Do you save a lot of money? If no, why not? If yes, how?

Yes/No, I _____.

→ Now give your partner some advice for saving money.

I think you're overspending, and you really should

_____.

7 With a partner, match the sentences to the pictures. Then choose a picture and create a short dialogue. Share your dialogue with the class.

1 _____ You spend too much money!

2 _____ How much do you make each month?

3 _____ I don't have enough money to pay the bills!

VI Now, Time to Pronounce!

Pitch Words 音高

When you change pitch, you make your voice higher or lower. Changing the pitch of a word can give that word extra meaning. 如果改變聲調，聲音會變得比較尖或低沉。一個字的聲調如果改變，可能含有其他的意義。

(088) **8** High pitch ▶ shows that a word is the main topic of your conversation.

How much do you spend on **essentials** each month?

I spend $1,000 on **rent** and $200 on **utility** bills.

You can also use a high pitch to make clear what you're asking about in a yes-no question.

Do **you** think it's important to save money? • *(I know that Jimmy thinks so, but do YOU?)*

(089) **9** Extra-high pitch ▶ makes a word sound dramatic.

I'm **really** in trouble this month. My landlord is going to **kill** me.

(090) **10** Rising pitch ▶ emphasizes your opinion.

A | I saved three hundred dollars this month.

B | That's a lot of money.

A | Hmm . . . It's **OK**, but it's not a **lot**.

(091) **11** Scoop pitch ▶ expresses uncertainty.

A | Have you saved a lot of money this month?

B | I've saved a **hundred** dollars. •

(Do you think that's A LOT?)

(092) **12** Read the following conversation. Draw the kind of pitch you think is needed above or below the words in bold. Then listen and check your answers.

A | How much do you spend on **luxury** items each month?

B | Well . . . I spend about $400 on **shoes** . . . are **they** luxury items?

A | What do **you** think they are?

B | I think shoes are **essentials**.

A | **Really**? I **can't** believe you think that!

Asking Someone Out 約會

I. Topic Preview

1 Flirting/pickup lines 調情／搭訕用語

Wow! You're gorgeous. Can I buy you a drink?

Sure, handsome. Wow! You look so strong. Have you been working out?

Do you believe in love at first sight, or should I walk by again?

That's so cheesy!

2 Asking someone on a date 邀某人約會

It was really nice talking to you. Let's get together again sometime.

I'd like that. Let me give you my number.

I was wondering if you'd like to go out to dinner with me this Saturday.

Sure, that sounds great. Where are you taking me?

I know a great little Italian restaurant. Can I pick you up at eight?

I'm looking forward to it.

3 Describing yourself 描述自己

I'm quite shy. I'm not the kind of guy who often asks girls out on dates.

I'm a Scorpio, so I'm very passionate. Are you a Pisces? I think we're compatible.

4 Turning someone down 拒絕某人

That pickup line is so cheesy!

I just don't think we're compatible.

I prefer guys who are tall, dark, and handsome.

Sorry, you're not my type.

II. Vocabulary & Phrases

P = Personality 個性
C = Compatible with 速配星座

Aquarius
水瓶座

P Friendly 友善
C Gemini 雙子座

Pisces
雙魚座

P Creative 富創造力
C Cancer 巨蟹座

Aries
牡羊座

P Competitive 好勝
C Leo 獅子座

Taurus
金牛座

P Loyal 忠誠
C Virgo 處女座

Gemini
雙子座

P Funny 有趣
C Libra 天秤座

Cancer
巨蟹座

P Caring 有愛心
C Scorpio 天蠍座

Leo
獅子座

P Generous 慷慨
C Sagittarius 射手座

Virgo
處女座

P Thoughtful 細心
C Capricorn 摩羯座

Libra
天秤座

P Charming 有魅力
C Aquarius 水瓶座

Scorpio
天蠍座

P Passionate 熱情
C Pisces 雙魚座

Sagittarius
射手座

P Optimistic 樂觀
C Aries 牡羊座

Capricorn
摩羯座

P Hardworking 勤奮
C Taurus 金牛座

Sentence Patterns

Pickup lines 搭訕用語

- Do you believe in love at first sight, or should I walk by again?
- Did it hurt when you fell out of heaven?
- Is it hot in here or is it just you?
- I hope you know CPR, because you take my breath away.
- If I could rearrange the alphabet, I'd put U and I together.
- Do I know you? Because you look a lot like my next girlfriend.

Asking someone out 邀某人約會

- It was really nice talking to you. Let's get together again sometime.
- Can I get your number? I'd love to take you out sometime.
- Would it be OK if I asked you out sometime?
- I was wondering if you'd like to go out to dinner with me this Saturday.
- Are you free this Saturday? I know a great cocktail bar where we can have drinks.
- If you don't have anything planned tonight, I'd love to take you to a movie.

1 Listen to the following conversations. Match each one to the picture that best illustrates it.

(096) 1 _____ 2 _____ 3 _____ 4 _____

(097) → Listen again and fill in the blanks.

1 Hey there, beautiful. I hope you know CPR, because you _____.

That's so _____.

2 Can I get your number? I'd love to _____ sometime.

Yeah, I'd like that. _____ write it down for you.

3 I know a great restaurant _____ we can have dinner.

What time do you want to _____?

4 Excuse me. Do I know you? Because you _____ my next girlfriend.

That pickup line is so _____.

74

② Fred is calling Jenna to ask her out. Listen to Fred's message.

(098) Check ☑ the correct words in his message.

Hi, Jenna. It's Fred. We met at the **1** **ⓐ** ☐ park **ⓑ** ☐ library yesterday. It was really

nice **2** **ⓐ** ☐ meeting **ⓑ** ☐ talking to you, and I was **3** **ⓐ** ☐ hoping **ⓑ** ☐ wondering if

you'd like to go out with me sometime.

If you don't have anything **4** **ⓐ** ☐ to do **ⓑ** ☐ planned this Friday,

I'd **5** **ⓐ** ☐ like **ⓑ** ☐ love to take you to this great **6** **ⓐ** ☐ restaurant **ⓑ** ☐ cocktail bar

I know. Maybe we can have **7** **ⓐ** ☐ dinner **ⓑ** ☐ drinks and get to know each other better.

I'm not the kind of guy **8** **ⓐ** ☐ that often **ⓑ** ☐ who usually asks girls out on dates, so

sorry if I sound a bit **9** **ⓐ** ☐ strange **ⓑ** ☐ nervous. Anyway, give me a call

and **10** **ⓐ** ☐ tell me **ⓑ** ☐ let me know what you think, all right? Bye!

IV. Now, Grammar Time!

Relative Clauses 關係子句
with
who, which, that, and where

Relative clauses give more information about a person, thing, or place. Introduce a relative clause with either a relative pronoun (*who, which, or that*) or a relative adverb (*where*).

我們用關係子句來替人、事物或地點補充額外資訊。關係子句會以關係代名詞（who、which、that）或關係副詞（where）開頭。

who *people* 人	I have a <u>friend</u> who *is very funny.*
which *things* 事物	The <u>message</u> which *you left on my voicemail was really sweet.*
that *people or things* 人或事物	I'm the kind of <u>guy</u> that/who *likes going out and having fun.* The <u>date</u> that/which *I went on last night was great.*
where *places* 地點	I know a great <u>restaurant</u> where *we can have a romantic dinner.*

❸ Pair Work! Choose a star sign from **Part II**. Describe yourself to your partner using "who" or "that." Can your partner guess your star sign?

 Example  GEMINI

GEMINI

Personality: Funny
Compatible with: Libra

LIBRA

Personality: Charming
Compatible with: Aquarius

A	I'm a person / I'm someone / I'm the kind of person who **likes to make jokes**. I'm compatible with people that **are likable and charming**.
B	Are you a **Gemini**?
A	Yes, I am.

 Repeat the exercise with different star signs.

4 Look at the following places. Take turns describing them using the model below.

Pedro's

True Flavor

Alleyway

Central Park

Club 100

Fisherman's Warf

 Pedro's is a place where **you can have a romantic dinner**.

 True Flavor is a place where _____.

- *you can get a nice cocktail*
- *you can have drinks with your friends*
- *you can take someone on a first date*

5 Match the statements on the left with those on the right. Write **who**, **which**, or **where** in the space given.

1 That pickup line _____ ...

2 He's the guy _____ ...

3 Let's go someplace _____ ...

4 I'm not the kind of girl _____ ...

5 Sorry, the phone number _____ ...

a we can have a drink together.

b will go out with just any guy.

c you just used was so cheesy.

d I gave you was wrong.

e took me to dinner last week.

6 Look at the pictures. Select one sentence from each box to form a three-sentence dialogue between two people.

A	Are you free this weekend?
B	Yes, I am. Where are you taking me?
A	I know a great place where we can have a romantic dinner.

A
- Hi, gorgeous! You're looking beautiful today!
- Do you believe in love at first sight, or should I walk by again?
- Are you free this weekend?
- I'd love to take you out sometime.

B
- Oh my God! You're so lame!
- I'm free this Saturday.
- You're funny. I like a guy with a sense of humor.
- Sorry, you're not my type.
- Yes, I am. Where are you taking me?

A
- I know a great place where we can have a romantic dinner.
- Great! I'll pick you up at eight.
- Then I'm your kind of guy!
- Please, just let me take you out on one date.

7 Pair Work! Listen to the following conversation and then practice it with a partner.

(099) Replace the words in color with ones from the word bank.

WORD BANK

- 💔 Would you like to dance?
- 💔 Can I get your number?
- 💔 Is it hot in here or is it just you?
- 💔 Did it hurt when you fell out of heaven?
- 💔 Can I buy you a drink?
- 💔 We should go out sometime.

- 💔 No, thanks.
- 💔 I don't think we're compatible.
- 💔 I don't like guys who use pickup lines.
- 💔 Yeah, I'd like that.
- 💔 Sure.
- 💔 Sorry, you're not my type.
- 💔 Sorry, I prefer guys who are taller.
- 💔 Oh my God! That's so cheesy!

- ♊ Gemini
- ♓ Pisces
- ♒ Aquarius
- ♏ Scorpio
- ♈ Aries
- ♋ Cancer
- ♌ Leo

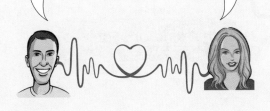

Man	*Hey there. Can I buy you a drink?*
Woman	*Sure.*
Man	*What's your star sign?*
Woman	*I'm a Pisces. Let me guess. Are you an Aries?*
Man	*Yeah, you're right. We should go out sometime.*
Woman	*Sorry, you're not my type.*

Pair Work! Follow the arrows. Ask and answer the questions.

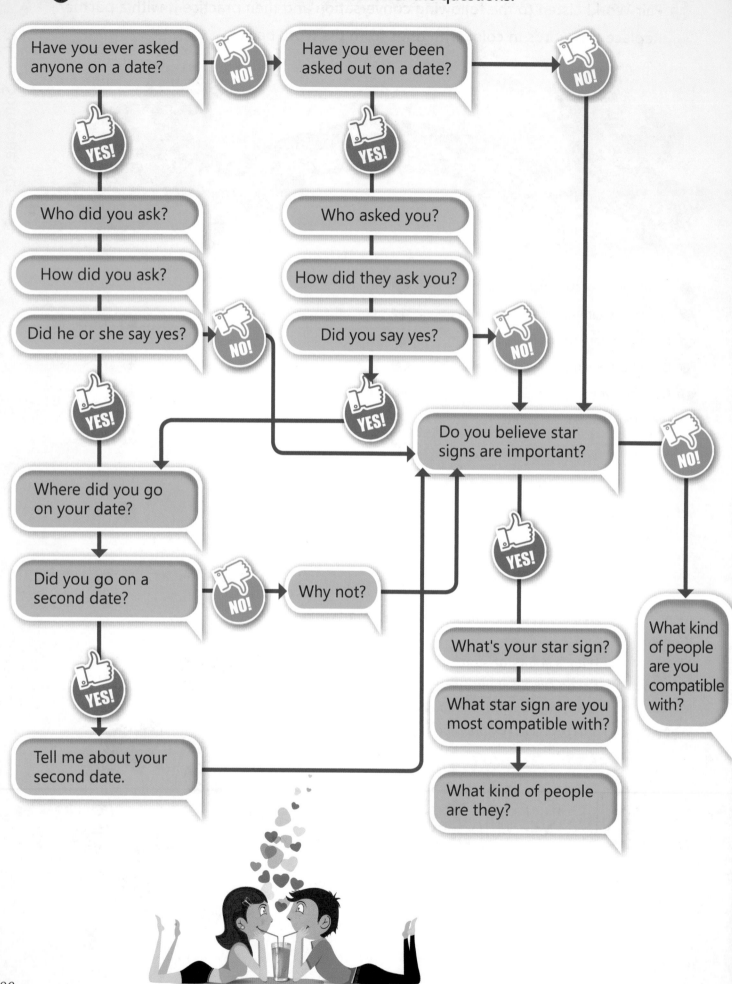

Have you ever asked anyone on a date?

NO!

Have you ever been asked out on a date?

NO!

YES!

YES!

Who did you ask?

Who asked you?

How did you ask?

How did they ask you?

Did he or she say yes?

NO!

Did you say yes?

NO!

YES!

YES!

Where did you go on your date?

Do you believe star signs are important?

NO!

Did you go on a second date?

NO!

Why not?

YES!

YES!

What's your star sign?

What kind of people are you compatible with?

Tell me about your second date.

What star sign are you most compatible with?

What kind of people are they?

80

Ⅵ. Now, Time to Pronounce!

Stress with Compound Nouns 複合名詞的重音

Compound nouns are nouns that are made up of two or more words
(e.g., blackboard, swimming pool, brother-in-law, etc.).
複合名詞是由兩個以上的單字組成的名詞（例如：黑板、游泳池、小叔／小舅子）。

9 With compound nouns, the stress usually comes on the first word.
(100) Listen and repeat the following words.

| **black**board | **foot**ball | **ten**nis racket | **hair**cut | **pick**up line |

10 Look at the pictures and repeat the words. Pay attention to the stress.

(101)

a white board 白色的板子 | a **white**board 白板 | a black bird 黑色的鳥 | a **black**bird 八哥

a green house 綠色的房子 | a **green**house 溫室 | a red head 紅色的頭 | a **red**head 紅髮的人

11 Listen to the sentences and match each one to the picture that best describes it.

(102)　**1** _____　**2** _____　**3** _____　**4** _____

81

Deadlines
截止期限

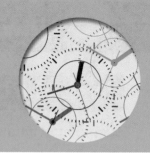

I. Topic Preview 103

1 Meeting a deadline 在截止期限內完成

When do you have to finish the project by?

The deadline is 5:00 p.m. Tuesday.

Do you think you'll meet the deadline?

Yes, I think so. I'm on schedule.

2 Talking about consequences of missing a deadline 談論超過截止期限的後果

Why do you look so worried?

If I don't finish this by noon, it'll cost the company a lot of money.

How's the report going? Almost finished?

No, I'm having some problems with it. It's taking longer than I expected.

Come on. I need this done by noon. Time is money.

3 Estimating how long it will take to finish an assignment 預估完成一件工作的時間

How much longer is it going to take you to finish the presentation?

I need to spend a few more hours working on it. Sorry.

4 Negotiating a deadline extension 協商延後截止日期

Would it be possible to get an extension on my deadline? I'm really snowed under right now.

OK. How about I give you until Monday?

That would be great. I should be able to finish it by then.

II. Vocabulary & Phrases 🎧104

paperwork
文書工作

project 計畫

presentation 簡報

essay 論文

report 報告

deadline 截止期限

extension 延長

**be on schedule /
be on track**
按照預定時間進行／
依照計畫進行

be behind
進度落後

**be snowed under /
be up to (one's) ears**
忙不過來／忙得不可開交

slack off 懈怠

procrastinate 延遲

make excuses 找藉口

edit 編輯

proofread 校對

Sentence Patterns 🎧105

• When do you have to finish *your project* by? /
When's the deadline for *your project*? /
When's *your project* due?
I have until *5:00 p.m.* on *Tuesday* to finish it. /
I have to finish it by *5:00 p.m.* on *Tuesday*. /
The deadline is *5:00 p.m.* on *Tuesday*. /
It's due by *5:00 p.m.* on *Tuesday*.

• Do you think you'll meet the deadline? /
Do you think you'll finish in time?
I don't think I'll be able to finish it by the deadline.

• If I don't finish the *report* by *noon*, *I'll get fired*.

• I need this done by *2:00 p.m.* /
I need you to finish this by *2:00 p.m.*

• I'll (definitely) have it done by *Thursday*. /
I should be able to finish it by *this afternoon*.

• Time is money. / Pull your socks up. /
Quit *slacking*. / Chop-chop!

• How much longer is it going to take you to finish *the paperwork*?
I need to spend *a few more hours working on it.* /
It's going to take me *a few more hours to finish it*.

• Would it be possible to get an extension on my deadline? /
Could you give me a little more time to finish?

• I'm behind right now.
How about I give you until *Monday*? /
Can you finish it by *Monday*?

1 Look at the topics below. Write down which ones you hear in each of the following
(106) conversations. The first one has been partly done for you.

a Meeting a deadline

b The consequences of missing the deadline

c Estimating how long it will take to finish

d Getting an extension

SCHEDULE

1 _c, b,_   **2** _____   **3** _____   **4** _____

(107) Read the questions below. Then listen again and check ☑ the correct answer.

1
- The deadline for the report is **a** ☐ in two hours **b** ☐ at two o'clock.
- The woman is **a** ☐ on schedule to finish the report **b** ☐ behind in finishing the report.
- If the woman doesn't finish the report, the boss will **a** ☐ fire her **b** ☐ get mad.

2
- Sam's deadline is **a** ☐ 12 o' clock **b** ☐ one o'clock on **a** ☐ Monday **b** ☐ Friday.
- Sam thinks he will **a** ☐ meet **b** ☐ miss the deadline.
- At the moment, Sam is **a** ☐ very busy **b** ☐ procrastinating.

3
- John **a** ☐ has **b** ☐ hasn't finished his **a** ☐ project **b** ☐ report.
- It will take John about an hour to **a** ☐ proofread **b** ☐ finish his work.

4
- Will **a** ☐ makes an excuse **b** ☐ asks for an extension when he sees the professor.
- The professor suggests **a** ☐ a new deadline **b** ☐ that Will stop slacking.
- If Will doesn't hand in the **a** ☐ essay **b** ☐ report by Tuesday,

  he'll **a** ☐ fail **b** ☐ get an extension.

2 Listen to the following conversation. Check ☑ the picture that best illustrates it.

🎧108

Ⓐ ☐ Ⓑ ☐ Ⓒ ☐ Ⓓ ☐

➡ 🎧109 Read the phrases below first, and then listen again. Check ☑ the phrases that you hear.

a ☐ I'm on track.

b ☐ I'm a little behind.

c ☐ The deadline is this afternoon.

d ☐ I need it done by 2:00 p.m.

e ☐ You need to get it done chop-chop!

f ☐ Quit slacking and get back on schedule.

g ☐ I'm snowed under right now.

h ☐ How much longer is it going to take?

i ☐ You need to stop making excuses and pull your socks up.

j ☐ I'll definitely have it done by the deadline.

3 Listen to the first half of each conversation and fill in the blanks. Then match each one to the best response.

🎧110

1 How _____ is it _____ _____ to finish? •

2 _____ the _____, but I need to _____ some _____ it. •

3 _____ your essay _____? _____ it _____ again? •

4 _____ it be _____ to _____ an _____? •

5 I really _____ it _____ this afternoon. _____ you _____? •

• a How about I give you until Monday evening to finish it?

• b Time is money, Tim. Chop-chop!

• c Don't worry. I'll definitely have it done by then.

• d It'll probably take me another three hours.

• e The deadline is tomorrow. I'm really behind.

85

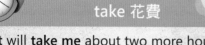 

IV. Now, Grammar Time!

take, spend, cost, pay

take 花費

- It will **take me** about <u>two more hours</u> **to finish** the essay.
- **Finishing the report** is going to **take me** <u>all day</u>.
- I **took** <u>three hours</u> **to finish** the essay.

spend 花費

- I need to **spend** about <u>half an hour</u> **edit**ing the report.
- I **spent** <u>all day</u> **on** that essay.
- The boss **spent** <u>$200</u> **buy**ing a new printer for the office.
- I want to **spend** <u>my bonus</u> **on** a new smartphone.

cost 花費

- **This delay** will **cost** the company <u>$10,000</u>.
- It **cost** (me) <u>$100</u> **to fix** my computer.

pay 支付

- The company **pays** me <u>$2,000</u> a month **to work** for them.
- I **paid** <u>$600</u> **for** that new sofa.

❹ Pair Work! Practice the short dialogues below. Fill in the blanks with the correct form of *take*, *spend*, *cost*, or *pay*, and any other words you think are necessary.

1
A   How much longer is _____ going to _____ you _____ finish your essay?

B   It is going to _____ about another hour to finish.

A   OK. Remember you need to proofread it, too.

B   I'll _____spend_____ some time _____ it after I've finished.

2
A   How much time did you _____ on that report, Joe?

B   I _____ about two hours _____ it.

A   Really good work. I don't think this company _____ you enough.

B   Thank you, Mr. Price.

3
A   Buying new computers for the office _____ us a lot of _____ last year.

B   We'll definitely need to _____ less money this year.

A   We also _____ over $10,000 for a new copy machine.

B   Well, it _____ a lot of money _____ run a successful business.

4
A   Have you finished your presentation?

B   Yes, but I want to _____ some time editing it.

A   Will that _____ long?

B   No. _____ it will only _____ me about half an hour.

V. Now, Time to Speak!

5 Pair Work! Listen to the dialogues and practice them with a partner. Then use the prompts to have similar conversations.

111

A

Woman	When's the deadline for your **project**?
Man	I have until **12:00 p.m. on Monday** to finish it.
Woman	Do you think you'll finish in time?
Man	**Yeah, I think so. I'm on schedule.**

B

Man	How's the **essay** going, Emily?
Woman	**Not so good. I'm a little behind at the moment.**
Man	Don't forget that I need it done by **12:00 p.m. on Monday**.
Woman	OK. I'll definitely have it done by then.

1

DEADLINE
this afternoon

2

DEADLINE
tomorrow morning

3

DEADLINE
noon on Wednesday

4

DEADLINE
3:00 p.m. today

5

DEADLINE
lunchtime

6

DEADLINE
10:00 a.m. on Tuesday

6 With your partner, decide how to fill in the blanks below. Discuss your answers with the class. Then practice the dialogue.

Common excuses 常見藉口

I can't concentrate. 我無法專注。	I'm finding it hard to focus. 我發現很難集中注意力。	I'm always getting distracted. 我老是分心。	I'm drawing a blank. 我一無所獲。	I keep hitting a wall. 我遇到瓶頸。

Mr. Jones	Have you almost finished your _____, Simon?
Simon	Sorry, Mr. Jones. I'm _____.
Mr. Jones	Well, _____, so get it done chop-chop!
Simon	Sorry, Mr. Jones. I'll try, but I'm _____.
Mr. Jones	Simon, quit _____. If you don't _____ _____.
Simon	_____ get an extension?
Mr. Jones	Hmm. How _____?
Simon	_____.
Mr. Jones	OK. Have it on my desk by _____.

7 With your partner, choose two sentences to go with each of the pictures below. Then use one of the pictures to create a short conversation that includes the phrases.

a "I'm on schedule."

b "How much longer is it going to take you to finish?"

c "How about I give you until next Monday?"

d "I need it done by this afternoon."

e "If you don't finish it in time, it'll cost the company a million dollars!"

f "I'm up to my ears in other work at the moment."

VI. Now, Time to Pronounce!

Vowel Sequences 連續母音

A vowel sequence is when one vowel sound directly follows another.
Here are some of the most common vowel sequences:
當一個母音緊接著另一個母音時，就構成了連續母音。以下是一些最常見的連續母音：

8 [aʊ] [aɪ] [o] [e] [ɔɪ] + [ə] or [ɚ]

🎧 112 Listen and repeat the words that you hear.

riot [`raɪət ]    power [ `paʊɚ]   royal [`rɔɪəl]

player [`pleɚ ]    slower [ `sloɚ]

🎧 113 Listen to the words. Do you hear a vowel sequence?
Check ☑ the sound that you hear.

1 ⓐ □ [aɪə]	**2** ⓐ □ [ɔɪɚ]	**3** ⓐ □ [aʊɚ]	**4** ⓐ □ [oɚ]	**5** ⓐ □ [eɚ]
ⓑ □ [aɪ]	ⓑ □ [ɔɪ]	ⓑ □ [aʊ]	ⓑ □ [o]	ⓑ □ [e]
6 ⓐ □ [aʊɚ]	**7** ⓐ □ [eɚ]	**8** ⓐ □ [aɪə]	**9** ⓐ □ [ɔɪɚ]	**10** ⓐ □ [oɚ]
ⓑ □ [aʊ]	ⓑ □ [e]	ⓑ □ [aɪ]	ⓑ □ [ɔɪ]	ⓑ □ [o]

9 vowel + [ɪŋ]

🎧 114 Listen and repeat the words that you hear.

being [`biɪŋ ]    doing [ `duɪŋ]   knowing [`noɪŋ]

flying [`flaɪɪŋ ]    drawing [ `drɔːɪŋ]

🎧 115 Listen to and repeat each of the following words.
Then add –ing and say each word aloud.

1 see		**2** enjoy		**3** say		**4** claw
5 bow		**6** go		**7** glue		**8** annoy

🎧 116 Listen again and check your pronunciation.

Getting Rid of Bad Habits 改掉壞習慣

I. Topic Preview 117

1 *Telling someone they have a bad habit* 指出對方的壞習慣

Some people have complained about you biting your nails at your desk.

What? I don't bite my nails, do I?

Could you stop cracking your knuckles? It's driving me crazy.

I'm so sorry. I'll try to stop myself in future.

2 *Giving advice to someone with a bad habit* 針對別人的壞習慣給予建議

How can I break this habit?

Maybe you could try replacing your habit with another action.

How did you quit smoking?

I went to see a hypnotist, and he cured me.

3 *Admitting you have a bad habit* 承認你有壞習慣

OK. I admit it. I'm addicted to Facebook.

I guess I do sometimes eavesdrop when I'm lonely.

4 *Explaining why you have this habit* 說明為何養成此壞習慣

If you don't go on Facebook, how do you feel?

I feel really agitated and nervy. I just can't help myself.

5 *Giving someone an ultimatum* 下最後通牒

If you don't quit picking your nose, I'm going to have to break up with you.

I'll do my best to stop.

II. Vocabulary & Phrases 〔118〕

talk with one's mouth full 嘴裡有東西時說話

drumming one's fingers 用手指敲桌子

crack one's knuckles 折手指關節

roll one's eyes 翻白眼

eavesdrop 偷聽

talk to oneself 自言自語

(go on) social networks （上）社群網站

(play) online games （玩）線上遊戲

(watch) soap operas （看）肥皂劇

see a hypnotist/therapist 看催眠師／治療師

distract oneself by doing something 分心做其他事情

replace A with B 用 B 取代 A

calm 平靜的

lonely 寂寞的

agitated 激動的

Sentence Patterns 〔119〕

- *Lots of people* have complained about you *biting your nails.* /
  Could you stop *cracking your knuckles*? It's *driving me crazy*. /
  It's really *annoying* when you *roll your eyes* like that.
- I didn't even realize I was doing it. /
  I don't *talk with my mouth full*, do I?
- How can I break this habit? /
  Can you give me any tips on how to stop *swearing*?
- Maybe you could/should try replacing *your habit with something else*. /
  I went to see a *hypnotist*, and he cured me.

- I admit it. I'm addicted to *(watching) soap operas*. /
  I guess I do sometimes *have a cigarette* when I'm *stressed*.
- If you don't *crack your knuckles*, how do you feel?
  If I don't *crack my knuckles*, I feel really *agitated*.
- Why do you think you *bite your nails*?
  Biting my nails makes me feel *calm*. /
  I usually *bite my nails* when I'm *nervous*.
- If you don't quit *picking your nose*, I'm going to have to *break up with you*.
- I'll try to stop myself in future. /
  I'll do my best to stop.

III. Now, Time to Listen!

1 Listen to the following conversation between Dom and Fran.
Number the events below in the order that you hear them.

(120)

a	_____	Dom gives Fran some advice on how to quit her bad habit.
b	_____	Fran admits she has a bad habit.
c	_____	Dom tells Fran she has a bad habit.
d	_____	Dom gives Fran an ultimatum.
e	_____	Fran tells Dom how her habit makes her feel.

STOP
BAD HABITS

(121) ➡ Listen again and check ☑ the correct word or phrase to complete what each person says.

1 A lot of our **a** ☐ friends **b** ☐ customers have complained about you

 a ☐ biting your nails **b** ☐ cracking your knuckles.

....

2 And if you don't **a** ☐ stop doing **b** ☐ quit it,

 I am going to have to **a** ☐ replace **b** ☐ fire you, I'm afraid.

....

3 I guess I do sometimes crack my knuckles when I'm **a** ☐ stressed **b** ☐ nervous.

....

4 Maybe you could try replacing it with **a** ☐ something else **b** ☐ another habit,

 like **a** ☐ doodling **b** ☐ taking deep breaths.

....

5 I'll **a** ☐ do **b** ☐ try my best to quit.

BAD HABITS

92

2 Listen to the first half of each conversation and match each one with the appropriate response.

(122)

1 •

2 •

3 •

4 •

5 •

• **a** Hmm. Maybe you could try seeing a therapist.

• **b** Is it really that bad? I think you're overreacting.

• **c** Finally! At least you've admitted it now.

• **d** I guess going on those sites makes me feel popular.

• **e** Sorry. I didn't even realize I was doing it.

3 Terry is asking Lisa for advice on giving up his bad habit. Listen to their conversation and complete the chart.

(123)

	Terry	Lisa	Tina
1 Who is addicted to online games?			
2 Who suggests that Terry distract himself with walking?			
3 Who broke his/her bad habit by getting a pet?			
4 Who used to talk to herself/himself?			
5 Who went to see a therapist?			
6 Who has already broken his/her bad habits?			

(124) ➡ Listen again and fill in the blanks with the phrases that Terry and Lisa say.

a _____ to online games, and I don't know how to give them up.

b Caring for a pet really _____ watching soaps.

c My friend Tina _____ to cure her bad habit.

d She _____ nonstop, but now she doesn't do it at all.

Reflexive Pronouns 反身代名詞	**Used when the subject and object are the same person/thing** **Used to emphasize "you and no one else"** 當主詞和受詞指同一個人或同一件事的時候使用 用來強調「獨力完成」
myself	I just can't control **myself**. (x) ~~I just can't control me.~~
yourself	**You** need to break this habit by **yourself**. *(you and no one else)*
himself	If he doesn't stop, **he**'s going to make **himself** ill.
herself	**She** won't admit to **herself** that she has a bad habit.
itself	**This habit** won't break **itself**.
ourselves	**We** need to be honest with **ourselves**.
yourselves	Why can't **you two** control **yourselves**?
themselves	**They** need to finish the job by **themselves**.

❹ Fill in the blanks in the following sentences with either a reflexive pronoun or an object pronoun (me, you, him, etc.).

1 I'll help them if they're willing to help _____.

2 It's OK. We can do it. You don't need to help _____.

3 She can't change because she doesn't believe in _____.

4 I can't help him. He'll have to figure it out by _____.

5 I went to see a hypnotist, and that really helped _____ quit smoking.

6 I want to stop, but I just don't know how to stop _____ from doing it.

7 Thanks for asking me, but I don't really know what advice to give _____.

8 Let me help you. Breaking a habit is a difficult thing to do by _____.

V. Now, Time to Speak!

5 Listen to the following conversations and practice them with your partner.

(125) A

Pam	Jim, this is a bit awkward, but some people have complained about you **eavesdropping on their conversations**.
Jim	Oh, I'm so sorry. I guess I do **eavesdrop** sometimes when I'm **bored**.
Pam	Well, thanks for admitting it. Maybe you could try **replacing eavesdropping with something else, like doodling**.
Jim	Yeah, OK. That's a good idea.

B

Erin	Pete, can you give me some tips on how to quit **smoking**?
Pete	OK. Let me ask you something. If you don't **smoke**, how do you feel?
Erin	I feel really **agitated** if I don't **have a cigarette**.
Pete	Hmm. Maybe you could try **seeing a hypnotist**?

➡ Now use the following pictures to create similar conversations.

a

going online all the time . . .

b

c

d

e

f

6 Pair Work! Look at the pictures of the people below. Choose one and discuss it with your partner. Talk about:

- The relationship between the people in the picture
- Who has the bad habit and what it is
- Why Person A performs the bad habit
- How Person B feels about Person A's behavior
- What ultimatum you think Person B would give person A
- What Person A should do to try to break his/her habit

7 Now decide how to fill in the blanks in the following dialogue. Practice the dialogue with your partner and then share it with the class.

A	Could you _____.
	It's really _____.
B	What? I didn't even know _____.
A	Well, if you don't _____, I'm going to have to
	_____.
B	OK. Well, what can I do to break the habit?
A	Let me ask you something. Why do you _____?
B	I usually do it _____.
A	OK. Then maybe you should try replacing _____,
	like _____.
B	That's not a bad idea. Thanks. I'll _____.

8 Role-Play! Choose one of the following scenarios and act it out with your partner.

- Student A is a therapist/hypnotist. Student B is someone who's trying to break a bad habit.

- Student A is someone looking for advice on how to break a habit.

  Student B is a friend with experience of breaking a bad habit.

- Student A is a boss who has to tell an employee (Student B) to stop performing a bad habit.

VI. Now, Time to Pronounce!

New-Information Stress 加重音於新資訊

9 When answering a WH-question, the tonic stress (see Unit 5) falls on the new information given.

(126) → Listen and repeat the sentences.

1 Why do you roll your eyes like that?
I roll my eyes when I'm annoyed.

2 How did you quit smoking?
I went to see a therapist.

3 Who here bites their nails?
Brenda bites her nails.

4 Why did Jen break up with you?
Because I couldn't stop eavesdropping.

10 Read the following sentences. <u>Underline</u> the words that you think should receive the new-information stress.

1 Who is going to tell Jack about his bad habit?

Jill is going to tell him.

2 Why do you watch so much TV?

Because I'm addicted to soap operas.

3 When are you leaving tomorrow?

I'm leaving at nine.

4 What's your most annoying habit?

My most annoying habit is smoking.

(127) → Now listen and check your answers.

The Technology Craze and Problems
科技狂熱和問題

I. Topic Preview

1 *Reporting and solving a problem with your computer* 描述和解決電腦問題

This is so frustrating! My computer keeps crashing, and I don't know why it's doing that.

Hmm. Maybe it's a virus. Have you run a system scan recently?

Do you know how to get my computer to run faster?

You could perform a disk cleanup. Try deleting your temporary Internet files.

2 *Talking about Internet habits* 談論上網習慣

What do you mostly use the Internet for?

Which search engine do you use?

Do you download a lot of movies from online stores?

I use it mostly for reading the news.

I usually use Google.

Yes, and music, too.

3 *Describing devices* 描述科技裝置

This is the newest model. It has an HD camera, 64 gigabytes of memory, and 4G.

4 *Annoyances* 惱人的事物

Stop using your smartphone all the time.

Sorry. I'm just checking the latest soccer results.

That phone has made you really antisocial.

Can you not use your phone while we're eating?

Sorry. I'm just texting my boss.

II. **Vocabulary & Phrases**

crash / freeze
當機

shut itself down
自動關機

RUNDLL
Error loading C:\WINDOWS\system32\ehkspkev.dll
The specified module could not be found.
OK

display an error message 顯示錯誤訊息

Temporary Internet files
Pages you view on the Internet are stored in a special folder for quick viewing later.
Delete Cookies... | Delete Files... | Settings...

delete the temporary Internet files
刪除網頁暫存檔

run slowly
速度很慢

virus 病毒

install antivirus software
安裝防毒軟體

run a system scan
執行系統掃瞄

operties | Uninstall or change a pro
▲ Hard Disk Drives (2)
OS (C:)
8.23 GB free of 134 GB
▲ Devices with Removable St
DVD RW Drive (E:)

full memory
記憶體已滿

Disk Cleanup for (C:)
Disk Cleanup
You can use Disk Cleanup to free up to 63.7 MB of disk space on (C:).
Files to delete:
☑ Downloaded Program Files — 0 bytes
☑ Temporary Internet Files — 11.0 MB
☐ Offline Webpages — 93.4 KB
☐ Recycle Bin — 14.9 MB
☐ Setup Log Files — 34.0 KB
Total amount of disk space you gain: 14.0 MB
Description

perform a disk/drive cleanup
執行磁碟／硬碟清理

low battery
電源不足

charge the battery
充電

turn it off and on again / restart it
重新開機

DOWNLOAD
download 下載

UPLOAD
upload 上傳

operating system
作業系統

Sentence Patterns

- My computer keeps *crashing*, and I don't know why. Maybe *the memory is full*. Have you *deleted the temporary Internet files* recently?
- Do you know how to get my computer to *stop shutting itself down*?
  You could *run a system scan*. /
  Try *charging the battery*.
- Which *social network* do you use?

- What do you mostly use the Internet for?
  I mostly use it for *doing research*.
- Do you *download* a lot of *apps*?
  (app [æp] = application)
- Stop *playing online games* all the time. /
  Having that *phone* has made you really *antisocial*.
- Can you not *text* while we're *talking*?
  Sorry. I'm just *texting my friend*.

1 Listen to Jimmy and Kate discuss their different smartphones. Which devices belong to Jimmy and Kate?

131

Jimmy : _____   Kate : _____

Network: 3G	Network: 4G	Network: 4G	Network: 3G
OS: Android 4.0	OS: Android 4.2	OS: iOS 6	OS: iOS 5
Memory: 16 GB	Memory: 16 GB	Memory: 64 GB	Memory: 64 GB
Card slot: Yes (up to 32 GB)	Card slot: Yes (up to 32 GB)	Card slot: No	Card slot: No
Camera: 13 MP	Camera: 16 MP HD	Camera: 8 MP HD	Camera: 8 MP

2 Use the pictures and context clues to fill in the blanks in the dialogues below. Use the words and phrases from the box.

🔍	tried turning it off	operating system	downloading	-megapixel HD camera	social network

🔍	error message	give me a hand	it have 4G	pay more attention	see your new smartphone

🔍	mostly use	just checking Facebook	chatting with my friends	using your phone	on that

1

Tony   Jenny, can you _____ for a second?

Jenny Sure, Tony. What's up?

Tony   My computer keeps displaying this _____ _____. Do you know what's wrong with it?

Jenny Hmm. I'm not sure. Have you _____ _____ and on again?

100

2

Bill	Can I _____?
Sandy	Yeah, sure. Here it is.
Bill	Wow! Nice. Does _____?
Sandy	Yeah, and a 13_____.
Bill	Wow! I bet it takes great pictures.
	Which _____ does it use?
Sandy	It uses iOS 6.

3

Deb	What do you _____ the Internet for, Pete?
Pete	I mostly use it for _____ TV shows. You?
Deb	I mostly use it for _____.
Pete	Oh, right. Which _____ do you use?
Deb	Google Plus. Are you _____?
Pete	No, sorry. I use Facebook.

4

Alice	John? John! Are you listening to me?
John	What? Yes, I am. Sorry. I'm _____ _____.
Alice	Stop _____ all the time. It's really rude.
John	Sorry. I'll _____.
Alice	You'd better. Having that phone has made you really antisocial.

(132) ➡ Now listen and check your answers. Circle any mistakes you made, and correct them.

3 Are the people below talking about problems, Internet habits, or annoyances? Write the correct answer and any key words that helped you make your decision.

(133)

a problems	**b** Internet habits	**c** annoyances

1 _____ ⬭

2 _____ ⬭

3 _____ ⬭

(134) ➡ Listen again. Put the photos in order from 1 to 5 so that they best describe the content of each conversation.

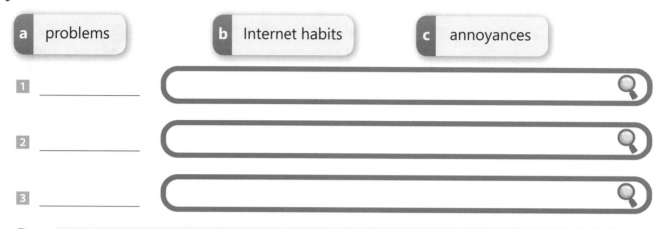

Problems

Internet habits

Annoyances

IV. Now, Grammar Time!

Indirect Questions
間接問句

Indirect questions often begin with: 間接問句通常以下列句型開頭：
❶ Can you tell me . . . ?
❷ Do you know . . . ?
❸ Do you have any idea . . . ?

Direct WH-Questions 直接 WH 問句	Indirect WH-Questions 間接 WH 問句
• **What** *is* the problem?	• Can you tell me **what** the problem *is*?
• **Why** *does* my computer *keep* crashing?	• Do you know **why** my computer *keeps* crashing?
• **When** *did* you last *charge* the battery?	• Can you tell me **when** you last *charged* the battery?
• **How** *do* I *stop* my phone from turning itself off?	• Do you have any idea **how to** stop my phone from turning itself off?

Direct Yes/No Questions 直接是非問句	Indirect Yes/No Questions 間接是非問句
• **Is** the memory **full**?	• Do you know *if* the memory **is full**?
• **Have** you **installed** any antivirus software?	• Can you tell me *whether* you **have installed** any antivirus software?
• **Will** I **be able to** take high-quality pictures with that camera?	• Do you know *if* I **will be able to** take high-quality pictures with that camera?

❹ Pair Work! Practice the dialogues. Change the questions in **bold** into indirect questions.

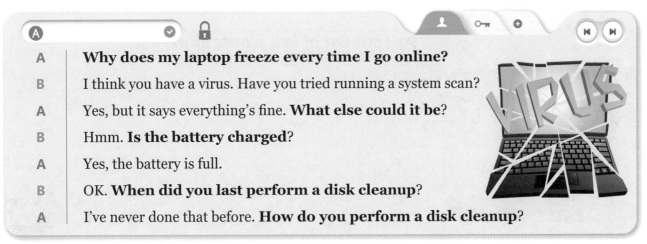

A	
A	**Why does my laptop freeze every time I go online?**
B	I think you have a virus. Have you tried running a system scan?
A	Yes, but it says everything's fine. **What else could it be**?
B	Hmm. **Is the battery charged**?
A	Yes, the battery is full.
B	OK. **When did you last perform a disk cleanup**?
A	I've never done that before. **How do you perform a disk cleanup**?

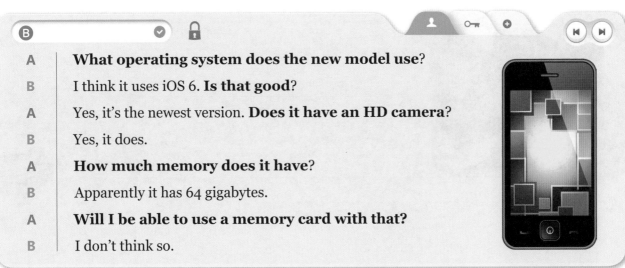

B	
A	**What operating system does the new model use**?
B	I think it uses iOS 6. **Is that good**?
A	Yes, it's the newest version. **Does it have an HD camera**?
B	Yes, it does.
A	**How much memory does it have**?
B	Apparently it has 64 gigabytes.
A	**Will I be able to use a memory card with that**?
B	I don't think so.

5 Look at the pictures and discuss them with your partner. Come up with a list of key words or phrases that the people in the pictures might use.

> ⚠ **Examples**   ✕
>
> Can you give me a hand?
>
> Can you take a look at my computer?
>
> My computer keeps crashing.
>
> You could try performing a disk cleanup.
>
> Try running a system scan.
>
> Maybe it's a virus.

➡ Now create short dialogues using your list to help you. Share your dialogues with the class.

▶ **Your list of key words or phrases:**

a

b

6 Listen to the dialogue and then discuss. Do you have a smartphone or a tablet? If so, describe it to your partner. If not, describe an electronic device you'd like to have.

(135)

Lucy	Is that your new smartphone?
Dan	Yeah. I got it just last month.
Lucy	Wow, it looks great! What make is it?
Dan	It's a Samsung Galaxy S4. It has 4G and an eight-megapixel HD camera.
Lucy	Nice! I bet it takes great videos. What operating system does it use? Android 4.1?
Dan	No, 4.2!
Lucy	Oh, right. And does it have 64 gigabytes of memory?
Dan	No, only 16, but I can use a memory card to get it up to 64.
Lucy	Cool. Actually I'm going to get a new smartphone next month.
Dan	Oh, yeah? Which model are you getting?
Lucy	I've got my eye on the new Sony, the Xperia Z Ultra.
Dan	I've heard of that. It's supposed to have a really good camera.
Lucy	Yeah, it's only got eight megapixels, but the quality is still supposed to be really good.
Dan	It also runs on Android 4.2, doesn't it?
Lucy	Yeah, and it has up to 64 gigabytes of memory with a memory card. But that's not the reason I want it.
Dan	No?
Lucy	No. The main reason I want it is because I love the design. It's so slim. It's only 6.5 millimeters thick!

7 Look at the picture sequences and use them to create dialogues.

Example

Chat ...

What do you mostly use the Internet for?

I mostly use it to download music. You?

I mostly use it to chat with my friends.

Oh, right. Which social network do you use?

I use Facebook.

Do you do a lot of online shopping?

Yes, I buy a lot of electronic books online.

+ ☺ *Write a message*   Send

❶

❷

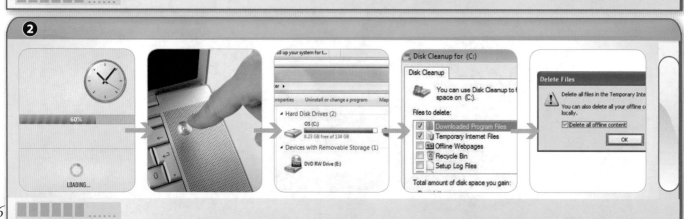

VI Now, Time to Pronounce!

Unstressed Words 非重音字

8 In Unit 4, you learned how the natural rhythm of English works. To keep the time between each stressed word the same, we have to say the unstressed faster than usual.

(136)

> We used to **go** to Ja**pan** every **su**mmer for our va**ca**tion.
>
> time 1 = time 2 = time 3 = time 4

To make unstressed words easier to say quickly, we can use the following techniques:
非重音字如果要唸得更順暢，可以使用下列技巧：

- Change the vowel sound to [ə] in certain words　有些字可以將母音改為 [ə]
- Create contractions　採用縮寫形式

(137) → Listen again to the above example.

Note　used to → [`justə]　　to → [tə]　　for → [fɚ]

9 Listen to and repeat the reduced words and common contractions.

(138)

you	[jə]	to	[tə]	have to	[`hæftə]	did you	[`dɪdʒə]
do	[də]	for	[fɚ]	has to	[`hæstə]	could you	[`kʊdʒə]
can	[kən]	and	[ən]	used to	[`justə]	would you	[`wʊdʒə]
a/an	[ə] / [ən]	the	[ðə]	do you	[djə]	would have (I would have)	[`wʊdə ] [ `aɪdə]

→ Now try saying the following sentences with the correct rhythm.

1 Could you please ask John to fix my computer?
2 What do you think the problem is?
3 Can you give me a hand for a minute?
4 I would have helped you if you'd asked.
5 Would you like me to give you some advice?
6 Why do you always have to text when we're eating?

(139) → Now listen and check your answers. Listen and repeat if necessary.

Going on a Diet
飲食控制

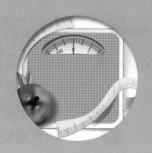

I. Topic Preview 140

1 Talking about your weight problems 談論體重問題

I really need to lose a few pounds.

Me, too. The older I get, the harder it is to stay in shape.

My problem is my lifestyle is really unhealthy. I never exercise.

My weakness is fatty foods. And I snack while I'm working.

2 Stating your goals 說出你的目標

I want to lose 20 pounds by this time next month.
I want to get rid of my love handles.
My goal is to get a flat stomach.

3 Explaining your diet 說明你的飲食

I have to avoid carbohydrates, and I'm only allowed to eat cabbage soup.

That sounds like a fad diet to me.

4 Discussing different ways to get thin
討論變瘦的各種方法

The best way to lose weight is to exercise.

I agree, but eating healthily is just as important.

5 Challenges and frustrations 挑戰與挫折

I've been dieting for weeks, but I just can't get rid of my gut.

When I was younger, I could eat anything and not put on weight. Now everything I eat goes straight to my thighs.

I find it really hard not to give in to temptation.

II. Vocabulary & Phrases

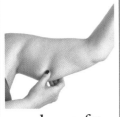
underarm fat
腋下脂肪（蝴蝶袖）

gut / belly
小腹

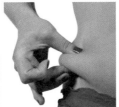
love handle
腰間贅肉

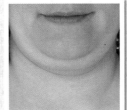
double chin
雙下巴

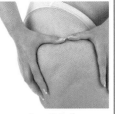
fat thigh
肥大腿

tone up (one's arms)
練（手臂）

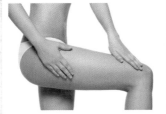
toned (thigh)
結實的（大腿）

six-pack / flat stomach
六塊肌／平坦的小腹

fad diet
極端的節食法

workout video
健身影片

give in to temptation
禁不起誘惑

(count) calories
（計算）卡路里

saturated fats
飽和脂肪

carbohydrates
碳水化合物

proteins
蛋白質

Sentence Patterns

- I really need to _tone up my stomach_.
- The _more stressed_ I get, the _faster_ I _put on weight_.
- My problem is _I eat too many carbohydrates_.
- My weakness is _ice cream_.
- I want to lose _100 pounds_ by _this time next year_.
- I want to get rid of my _fat thighs_. /
  My goal is to get _a really toned stomach_.
- I have to _avoid proteins_. /
  I'm (only) allowed _to eat 1,000 calories a day_. /
  I'm not allowed to _drink coffee_.

- The best way to lose weight is to _eat small regular meals_.
- _Exercising regularly_ is more important than _dieting_. /
  Eating healthily is just as important as _eating fewer calories_.
- I've _used 10 workout videos_, but I just can't _get rid of my love handles_.
- When I was younger I could _eat chocolate all day_ and not put on weight.
- Everything I eat goes straight to my _gut_.
- I find it really hard not to _snack while I'm working_.
- The worst thing about dieting is having to _count calories_.

1 Jane wants to go on a diet. Listen to her conversation with her friend Marty, and then answer the questions below.

143

1 What are Jane's goals?

a ☐   b ☐   c ☐   d ☐   e ☐

2 What does Marty think is the best way to lose weight?

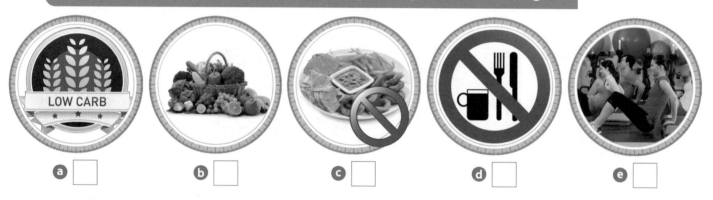

a ☐   b ☐   c ☐   d ☐   e ☐

3 Which of the following best illustrates Jane's current lifestyle?

a ☐   b ☐   c ☐

4 What does Marty suggest that Jane do?

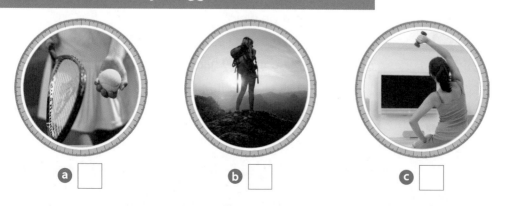

a ☐   b ☐   c ☐

2 Listen to the following people describe their dieting experiences. Fill in the diet center's progress sheet.

(144)

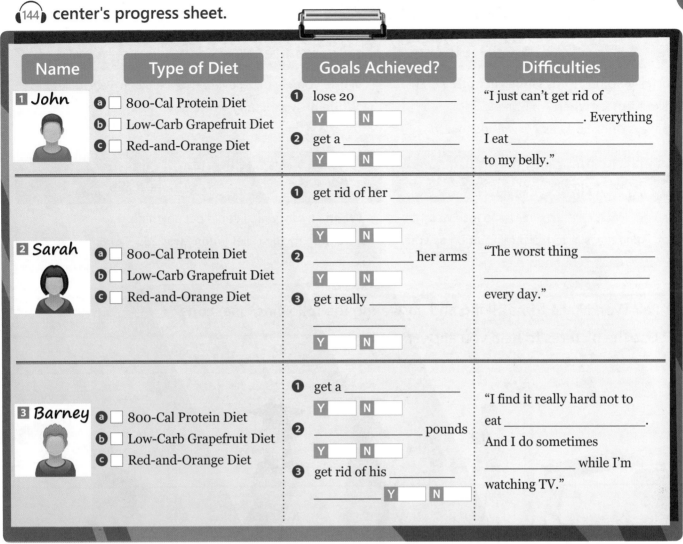

Name	Type of Diet	Goals Achieved?	Difficulties
1 John	**a** ☐ 800-Cal Protein Diet **b** ☐ Low-Carb Grapefruit Diet **c** ☐ Red-and-Orange Diet	**1** lose 20 _____ Y ☐ N ☐ **2** get a _____ Y ☐ N ☐	"I just can't get rid of _____. Everything I eat _____ to my belly."
2 Sarah	**a** ☐ 800-Cal Protein Diet **b** ☐ Low-Carb Grapefruit Diet **c** ☐ Red-and-Orange Diet	**1** get rid of her _____ _____ Y ☐ N ☐ **2** _____ her arms Y ☐ N ☐ **3** get really _____ _____ Y ☐ N ☐	"The worst thing _____ _____ every day."
3 Barney	**a** ☐ 800-Cal Protein Diet **b** ☐ Low-Carb Grapefruit Diet **c** ☐ Red-and-Orange Diet	**1** get a _____ Y ☐ N ☐ **2** _____ pounds Y ☐ N ☐ **3** get rid of his _____ _____ Y ☐ N ☐	"I find it really hard not to eat _____. And I do sometimes _____ while I'm watching TV."

3 Listen to Joan and Matt discuss their diets. Check ☑ the main topic of their conversation.

(145)

a ☐	Different ways to lose weight.	**b** ☐	Setting dieting goals.
c ☐	Overcoming dieting challenges.	**d** ☐	Fad diets.

➡ (146) Try to correct the following phrases from memory. Then listen and check your answers.

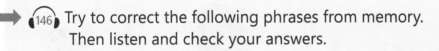

1 The ~~less~~ I eat, the more weight I put on.
    more

2 My problem is junk food.

3 I like to eat chocolate after I work out.

4 I find it really hard not to give in to laziness.

5 When I was a kid, I could eat anything and never get fat.

6 As we get older, it gets harder and harder to stay overweight.

IV. Now, Grammar Time!

Conjunctions of Time 表示時間的連接詞：
when, while, as

background actions 背景動作	simultaneous long actions 同時進行的較長動作
• I usually do push-ups **while** *I'm watching TV.* • I like to snack **when** *I'm working.* • I always drink soda **as** *I'm walking to work.*	• **While** you *ate* pizza every day, I *ate only vegetables.* • **While** he *was putting on* weight, I *was losing* it.
actions that change together 同時改變的動作	**ages and periods of life** 年齡和人生階段
• **As** you *get older*, it *gets harder* to lose weight. • You'll *find it easier* to resist temptation **as** you *become used to* your new diet.	• **When** *I was young*, I could eat anything. • I went on my first diet **when** *I was 25.*

④ Pair Work! Take turns asking and answering the following questions.
Use the pictures to help you answer.

a

When do you eat breakfast?

b

What happens to you as you get older?

c

When did you lose so much weight?

d

When do you usually eat chocolate?

e

What happens as you exercise?

f

What were you doing all morning?

g

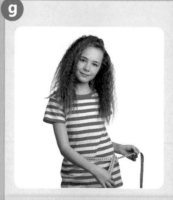

Were you overweight when you were a child?

h

What will happen as your diet improves?

V. Now, Time to Speak!

Popular Diets 常見的減肥法				
Cabbage Soup Diet 高麗菜湯減肥法	**Grapefruit Diet** 葡萄柚減肥法	**80-10-10 Diet** 80-10-10 減肥法	**Paleo Diet** 舊石器時代飲食法

80%

- Don't have bread, soda, or alcohol.
- Eat cabbage soup every day.
- Fruit, vegetables, and meat are sometimes allowed.

- Avoid carbohydrates.
- Eat half a grapefruit with every meal.
- Eat lots of fats and proteins.

- Eat 80% carbohydrates, 10% fat, and 10% protein.
- Eat only raw food.

- Do not have processed foods, sugar, salt, milk, cheese, coffee, or alcohol.
- Avoid potatoes.
- Eat lots of fruit and vegetables.

5 Pair Work! Use the chart above and decide how to fill in the blanks. Discuss your answers with the class. Then practice the dialogue.

A	Let me tell you about this new diet I'm on.
B	OK. What's it called?
A	It's called the _____.
B	And what does it involve?
A	Well, I have to _____, and _____ _____. I also have to _____ _____.
B	Hmm. I don't know. It sounds like a fad diet to me.
A	OK, well, what do you think is the best way to lose weight?
B	_____ and _____. But _____ is more important than _____.
A	Oh, but I hate _____!

6 Create a dialogue between the two people in the picture. Use the model as your starting point and the phrases in the box to help you.

Use the following phrases in your dialogue.

I really want to get rid of . . .

My goal is to . . .

My weakness is . . .

My biggest problem is . . .

I always . . . while . . .

I find it so hard (not) to . . .

My lifestyle is . . .

I hate . . .

The (more) I . . . , the (more) . . .

I really need to lose some weight.

Me, too.

The thing is that I've been dieting for weeks, but . . .

7 Take turns asking and answering the following questions.

🍎 Have you ever been on a diet?

🍎 Would you ever consider doing a fad diet? Why?

🍎 Are there any parts of your body you'd like to change?

🍎 What's your biggest weakness?

🍎 Do you have any bad eating habits?

🍎 Is your lifestyle healthy or unhealthy?

🍎 What do you think is the best way to lose weight?

VI. Now, Time to Pronounce!

Pitch Boundaries 聲調界線

The pitch boundary is the end of an intonation unit. Understanding pitch boundaries will let you know whether it's your turn to speak, or whether you should keep listening.
聲調界線是一組語調單位的結尾處，分辨聲調界線可以知道是否輪到自己說話，或者應該繼續傾聽。

8 **Falling pitch boundary 下降的聲調界線** A falling pitch boundary usually shows
(147) that the speaker has finished speaking. WH-Questions often have a falling pitch boundary, too. Listen and repeat.

1
A | What's your biggest weakness?
B | My biggest weakness is junk food.

2
A | What are your goals?
B | I want to get rid of my love handles.

Note that the pitch falls on the last stressed syllable of the unit.
注意聲調落在每組語調單位的最後一個重音節。

9 **Rising pitch boundaries 上升的聲調界線** Yes/No questions usually have a rising
(148) pitch boundary. A rising pitch boundary also shows that the speaker has not finished speaking yet. Listen and repeat.

A | Have you ever tried a fad diet?
B | Yes. I've tried the Grapefruit Diet, the Paleo Diet, and the Cabbage Soup Diet.
A | Is chocolate your biggest weakness?
B | Well, I like chocolate, but my biggest weakness is hamburgers.

10 Read the following conversation. Draw either a rising (↗) or falling (↘)
(149) intonation on the words in **bold**. Then listen and check your answers.

Jenny	Hi, **Tim**. How's your diet **going**?
Tim	It's going **OK**, but I'm having a few **problems**.
Jenny	Oh. Are you having trouble accomplishing your **goals**?
Tim	Yeah. I'm eating **healthily**; I'm **exercising**; but I've only accomplished one of my **goals**.
Jenny	Well, keep **at it**.
Tim	I don't know, **Jenny**. I think I should **quit**.
Jenny	Don't **give up**. Let me give you one of my **workout videos**.
Tim	Did it work for **you**?
Jenny	Yeah. I lost 20 pounds in a month with this **video**.

Dilemmas
抉擇

I. Topic Preview (150)

1 Narrowing down your choices 縮小選擇範圍

I don't know what to do after I graduate. I don't have any money to go traveling, so what should I do?

Let's look at your options. Since you don't have any money, you could either get a job or continue your studies.

2 Pondering which choice to make 思考該作何決定

Should I study for a master's degree, or should I take a gap year? I just can't decide.

I'm torn between studying English and studying math. Which one should I do?

3 Weighing up the pros and cons of a choice 衡量一項決定的優缺點

On the one hand, getting a car would be expensive. On the other, it would give me a lot of freedom.

Getting a tattoo is not only painful but also for life. But then again, tattoos are really cool.

4 Making your decision 作出決定

Have you made your decision?

Yes, I have. I've decided to run for election.

Why did you make that decision?

Because I think it'll be a good experience.

5 Asking for someone's advice 詢問他人意見

If you were me, what would you do in my situation?

If I were you, I would do neither.

II. Vocabulary & Phrases 🎧151

take a gap year
空檔年

do a master's degree
攻讀碩士學位

get a tattoo
刺青

run for election
參選

accept a job offer
接受一份工作

go speed dating
極速約會

major in a subject
主修某一學科

volunteer abroad
到國外當志工

gain life experience
獲得生活經驗

**earn money /
settle down**
賺錢／安頓下來

**open up career
opportunities**
開創職場契機

make a difference
有所作為

**a once-in-a-lifetime
experience**
一生一次的經驗

résumé
履歷

student government
學生會

Sentence Patterns 🎧152

- Let's *look at* your options. /
  Let's *try to narrow down* your options.
- Since *you don't have any money*, you should/could . . . /
  Seeing as *you already speak French*, it might be better to . . .
- You should/could either *major in modern languages* or *major in history*.
- Should I *do a master's degree*, or should I *take a gap year*? /
  I'm torn between *doing a master's degree* and *taking a gap year*.
- Let's weigh up the pros and cons.
- On the one hand, *you would gain some great life experience*. On the other hand, *it would be expensive*.

- *Doing a master's degree is* not only *hard work* but also *time consuming*.
- But then again, it would *look good on my résumé*.
- If you were me, what would you do?
  If I were you, I would *accept the job*.
- Have you made your decision?
  Yes, I've decided to *do a master's degree*.
  Why?
  Because I think it will *open up more career opportunities*. /
  Because it'll be a good chance to *gain life experience*.

1 Listen to the following conversation extracts. Match each one to the dilemma you think the people are discussing.

153

1 _____ 2 _____ 3 _____ 4 _____

a

b

c

d

2 Michael and Heidi are talking about their dilemmas. Fill in the blanks in their lists of pros and cons.

154

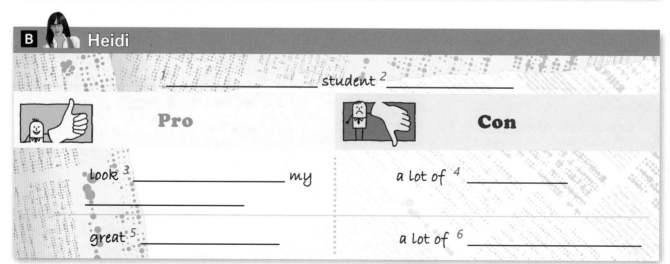

A Michael

Major in ¹ _____

👍 Pro	👎 Con
really ² _____	fewer career ³ _____

Major in ___business___

👍 Pro	👎 Con
⁴ _____	wouldn't ⁵ _____
career opportunities	_____ art

B Heidi

¹ _____ student ² _____

👍 Pro	👎 Con
look ³ _____ my _____	a lot of ⁴ _____
great ⁵ _____	a lot of ⁶ _____

3 Listen to the conversation between Joe and Sunny.
Check ☑ the correct phrase to complete each sentence.

(155)

1 Joe doesn't know where to **a** ☐ go for his birthday **b** ☐ take someone on a date.

2 Sunny narrows down his options to **a** ☐ two choices **b** ☐ three choices.

3 Sunny's advice is to go to **a** ☐ an art exhibition **b** ☐ an art-house movie.

4 Sunny is unsure if she should

a ☐ accept a job offer **b** ☐ start a master's degree or take a gap year.

5 Joe thinks taking a gap year is a good way to

a ☐ gain life experience **b** ☐ earn money.

6 Sunny thinks one of the **a** ☐ pros **b** ☐ cons of taking a gap year is how

a ☐ expensive **b** ☐ exciting it is.

(156) Now listen again and fill in the blanks with the phrases that Joe and Sunny say.

1 Let's _____ your _____.

2 I think you _____ to an art exhibition _____ to an

art-house movie.

3 If you _____, which one _____ you choose?

4 It'd _____ you something to talk about _____

give you a chance to impress her.

5 I'm _____ one this year and taking a gap year.

6 But _____, it would be really expensive.

7 _____ money is a problem,

it _____ to do the master's degree

right away.

8 But then again, it would be sad to _____

a _____ experience.

Correlative Conjunctions 關係連接詞
Use correlative conjunctions to join two ideas together.
用關係連接詞來連接兩個概念。

not only . . . but also 不僅……而且	• **Speed dating is fun + a good way to meet people.** → Speed dating is not only fun but also a good way to meet people. • **Speed dating is fun. + It's a good way to meet people.** → Not only is speed dating fun, (but) it's also a good way to meet people.
either . . . or 不是……就是	• **You could go to an exhibition / see a movie.** → You could either go to an exhibition or see a movie. • **You could go to an exhibition. / You could see a movie.** → Either you could go to an exhibition, or you could see a movie.
neither . . . nor 既不……也不	• **I wouldn't do a master's degree / take a gap year.** → I would neither do a master's degree nor take a gap year. • **Getting a tattoo / Buying a motorcycle is not a good idea.** → Neither getting a tattoo nor buying a motorcycle is a good idea.

4 Pair Work! Take turns asking and answering the following questions. Use the prompts given, along with *not only . . . but also*, *either . . . or*, and *neither . . . nor*.

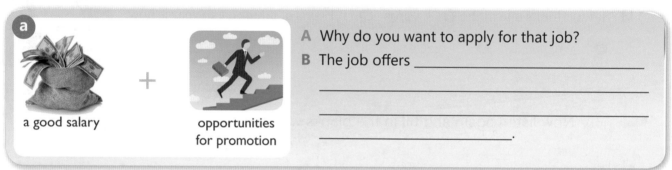

a

a good salary   +   opportunities for promotion

A Why do you want to apply for that job?
B The job offers _____
_____
_____
_____ .

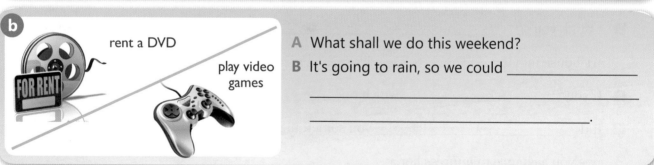

b

rent a DVD
play video games

A What shall we do this weekend?
B It's going to rain, so we could _____
_____
_____ .

c

painful   +   unprofessional

A If I were you, I wouldn't get a tattoo.
B Why not?
A _____ tattoos _____,
_____ they're _____
_____ .

d

confirm + deny

A Are you going to do a master's degree?

B I'm not sure. I can _____ _____ at the moment.

e

run for student president

run for welfare officer

A I want to run in the student government elections. What positions are still available?

B _____ you can _____ _____, _____ you can _____ _____.

f

go to Africa

go to Australia

A I want to go to either Africa or Australia on my gap year. What do you think?

B I would _____ _____. I would go to Europe.

V. Now, Time to Speak!

Here are some suggestions for line 1:

where to go on vacation this summer
what to buy my girlfriend for her birthday
what to do this weekend
what subject to major in next year
where to take my date

5 Pair Work! Listen to the dialogue and practice it with your partner. Then have a similar dialogue by replacing the words in bold with ideas of your own.

157

Barney	I don't know **what to do after I graduate**.
Robin	Let's look at you options. You could **get a job, take a gap year**, or do **a master's degree**.
Barney	Hmm. I don't want to **get a job yet**, but I'm torn between **taking a gap year** and **doing a master's degree**.
Robin	OK, let's weigh up the pros and cons.
Barney	Well, on the one hand, **taking a gap year** would be **expensive**, but on the other hand it'd **be a good chance to gain life experience**.
Robin	Yeah, and **doing a master's degree** is **a lot of work**. But then again, **it would look good on your résumé**. OK. Have you made a decision?
Barney	Yes, I've decided to **take a gap year** because I think it'll **be a once-in-a-lifetime experience**.

6 With your partner, take turns discussing the pros and cons of the following situations. Share your answers with the class. Did anyone think of anything different?

★ getting a tattoo
★ getting a part-time job
★ going speed dating
★ volunteering abroad
★ running for student president
★ major in art

More Vocabulary

★ challenging 有挑戰性的
★ a lot of responsibility 責任重大
★ time-consuming 費時的
★ embarrassing 使人尷尬的
★ give you an opportunity to . . . 提供……的機會

Examples

Not only is getting a tattoo painful, it's also . . .. But then again, it would look pretty cool.
On the one hand, getting a tattoo would be painful. But on the other, it would look . . .

7 Role-Play! Choose one of the subjects from Exercise 6. Student A needs Student B's help to decide whether to do it or not. Create a dialogue using the prompts below.

Student A	I don't know whether I should . . . or not. If you were me . . . ?
Student B	Well, personally, . . .
Student A	Why?
Student B	Because . . .
Student A	But . . .
Student B	OK. Seeing as . . .

VI. Now, Time to Pronounce!

Consonant Sequences 連續子音

🔍▾ Initial consonant sequences 字首的連續子音

$$[\,s\,] + [\,p, t, k, f, m, l, w\,]$$

8 Listen and repeat the words that you hear.

| space | stop | skill | sphere | small | slow | swim | suite |

→ (159) Listen and number the consonant sequences from 1 to 7 in the order that you hear them.

① [sp]	② [st]	③ [sk]	④ [sf]	⑤ [sm]	⑥ [sl]	⑦ [sw]
_____	_____	*1*	_____	_____	_____	_____

[p, t, k, b, d, g, f, θ, ʃ, v, n, m, h] + [l, r, w, j]

❾ Listen and repeat the words that you hear.

(160)

play	twin	cute	break	green	fewer
three	shrill	view	news	mute	huge

→ (161) Listen and fill in the blanks with the correct consonant sequence.

① [_____ æk]	② [_____ o]	③ [_____ ul]	④ [_____ ʊr]	⑤ [_____ aɪt]
⑥ [_____ ɛlv]	⑦ [_____ ɑm]	⑧ [_____ ik]	⑨ [_____ u]	⑩ [_____ ɛd]

🔍▾ **Final consonant sequences** 字尾的連續子音

❿ Here are some examples of common final consonant sequences.

(162) **Listen and repeat the words that you hear.**

stop + stop	stop + nasal	consonant + [θ]	nasal + consonant	consonant + [s, z, t, d]
fact	garden	wealth	jump	next
kept	written	fifth	thank	missed
rubbed	admit	strength	lunch	songs
dragged	top note	width	want	rats
blackbird	fragment	ninth	sums	best

→ (163) Now try saying the following sentences as fluently as possible. Then listen and check your pronunciation.

★ Please deliver milk to the fifth floor.

★ Help me change one of the flags to dark blue.

★ It's super fun to play catch in the small square.

★ Let's go to Europe next spring.

I. Topic Preview 🎧 164

1 *Talking about your education and your experience* 談論自己所受的教育和經歷

Tell me a little bit about your education.

And what about your work experience.

I attended Athena University, where I majored in graphic design.

I've worked for my current company for three years.

2 *Saying why you want the job*
說明應徵這份工作的原因

Why do you want to work for this company?

I feel like I'm ready for a new challenge.

3 *Talking about your strengths and weaknesses*
談論你的強項和弱點

Do you manage your time well?

Yes, I'm very organized.

What are some of your strengths?

My biggest strength is probably my communication skills.

4 *Discussing salary, work hours, and other conditions* 討論薪資、工時和其他條件

What kind of salary are you looking for?

I'm expecting something between $30,000 and $40,000.

Would traveling be a problem?

No, I'd be prepared to travel.

5 *Talking about your goals, expectations, and abilities* 談論你的目標、期許和能力

Where do you see yourself in five years?

In five years, I'd like to be a senior manager.

II. Vocabulary & Phrases 🎧165

manage (one's) time (well) / time-management skills

（善於）規劃時間／
規劃時間的能力

solve problems (well) / problem-solving skills

（善於）解決問題／
解決問題的能力

communicate (well) with others / communication skills

（善於）與人溝通／溝通技巧

lead others (well) / leadership skills

（善於）領導他人／
領導能力

work (well) as part of a team

（適合）團隊合作

handle responsibility / pressure

承擔責任／壓力

responsible

有責任感

attentive to detail / attention to detail

注重細節

creative / creativity

富有創意／創意

organized / organizational skills

有組織的／組織能力

show (one's) true potential

發揮真正的潛能

develop (one's) career

發展職業生涯

(enjoy a) challenge

（勇於接受）挑戰

work overtime

加班

start (one's) own business

創業

Sentence Patterns 🎧166

- Tell me a little bit about your education.
  I attended _Oxbridge_ University, where I majored in _English_.
- Tell me a little bit about your work experience.
  I've worked for _two different companies since I graduated_.
- Why do you want to work for this company? /
  Why did you apply for this position?
  I feel like _this job would give me a chance to develop my career_.
- Why should I hire you? /
  What makes you think you're suited to this job?
  My _leadership skills_ would be an asset to this company.
- Do you _handle responsibility well_? /
  Do you have the ability to _solve problems_? /
  Are you _attentive to detail_?
  I _handle responsibility well_. /
  I have _excellent_ _problem-solving skills_. /
  I am very _attentive to detail_.

- What are some of your strengths/weaknesses?
  My biggest strength is my ability to _lead others_. /
  My biggest strength is _my communication skills_.
- What kind of salary/pay range are you looking for?
  I'm expecting between _$40,000_ and _$50,000_.
- Would _traveling_ be a problem? /
  Would you be willing to _work long hours_?
  I'd be prepared to _travel_. / _Traveling_ suits me just fine. /
  I'd be more than ready to _work long hours_.
- Where do you see yourself in _five years_? What are your long-term goals?
  I'd like to _be a department head_.

1 Listen to the interview between Michael and Mrs. Peters, and check ☑ whether each
statement is true or false. Correct any false statements.

True	False	
☐	☐	**1** Michael went to college in Chicago.
☐	☐	**2** Michael majored in modern languages.
☐	☐	**3** Michael has worked as a tour guide, a reporter, and a translator.
☐	☐	**4** Michael has worked at his current job for about three years.
☐	☐	**5** Michael applied for this job because he wants a new challenge.

2 Listen to the second half of the interview. Check ☑ the pictures that best describe
Michael.

a ☐

b ☐

c ☐

d ☐

e ☐   improve

Read the phrases below. Then listen to the second half of the interview again and
check ☑ the phrases that you hear.

ⓐ	☐	What makes you think you're suited to this job?
ⓑ	☐	Why should I hire you?
ⓒ	☐	I think my communication skills will be a real asset to this company.
ⓓ	☐	My biggest strength is my ability to communicate well with others.
ⓔ	☐	I work really well as part of a team.
ⓕ	☐	I love working with other people.
ⓖ	☐	I don't manage my time very well.
ⓗ	☐	I think my biggest weakness is my time-management skills.
ⓘ	☐	I sometimes focus too much on one thing.
ⓙ	☐	I pay too much attention to details.

**Common Managerial Job Titles
常見管理職稱**

- CEO 總執行長
- Managing Director 董事總經理
- General Manager 總經理

- Department Head 部門主管
- Division Manager 部門經理
- Senior Manager 資深經理

- Team Leader 組長
- Assistant Manager 副理
- Supervisor 主管

3 Listen to the final part of the interview. Put the photos in order from 1 to 5 so that they best describe the content of the conversation.

170

a	b	c	d	e

171 ➡ Try to correct the following phrases from memory. Then listen again and check your corrections.

a I'd like to be a department head in five years' time.

b In the short term, my goal is to become CEO.

c So what kind of salary are you looking for?

d Do you like to travel?

e Traveling sounds just fine.

f I wouldn't be prepared to work long hours too often.

IV. Now, Grammar Time!

Two-Part Verbs 複合動詞：
phrasal verbs (verb + adverb)
短語動詞（動詞＋副詞）

Some phrasal verbs do not take a direct object. 有些短語動詞不能接直接受詞。

* Where did you **grow up**?
* I often **get up** before 7:00 a.m.
* Please, **sit down**.
* I like to **hang out** with my friends.

But some phrasal verbs take a direct object. 有些短語動詞可以接直接受詞。

* I **pick up** *new ideas* very fast.
* You need to **do** *this report* **over**.
* I never **put** *work* **off** until the last minute.
* Are you having trouble **carrying out** *your assignment*?
* I'm going to have to **turn** *your offer* **down**
* Why don't you take a few days to **think** *it* **over**?

 You can put the object between the verb and the adverb if you wish.
BUT if the object is a pronoun, you must put it in the middle.
也可以將受詞置於動詞和副詞之間。如果受詞是代名詞，則一定要置於中間。

Examples ▶ Why don't you **try out** *the job* for a month? → Why don't you **try** *the job* **out** for a month?

BUT Why don't you **try** *it* **out** for a month? ⊗ Why don't you <u>**try out**</u> *it* for a month?

---

4 **Pair Work! Practice the dialogues below. Use the prompts to make statements using phrasal verbs.**

> No, I turned it down. /
> No, I turned their offer down. /
> No, I turned down their offer.

A

Karen	Did you accept their offer?
Jack	(No / turned down) •
Karen	Why?
Jack	(thought over), but the salary was too low.

B

Chandler	Do you solve problems well?
Monica	(Yes / figure out) very quickly.
Chandler	And are you creative? Do you have many new ideas?
Monica	(Yes / think up) all the time.

C

Sheldon	There are a lot of mistakes in this report!
Penny	Sorry, boss. (will / do over)
Sheldon	OK, but do it now. Don't (put off) until later.

D

Lily	Tell me a little bit about yourself.
Marshall	Well, (grew up) in the country, and I moved to the city for college.
Lily	What did you major in?
Marshall	Oh, I didn't major in anything. (dropped out) after a year.

128

Two-Part Verbs: prepositional verbs (verb + preposition)
複合動詞：介系詞動詞
（動詞 + 介系詞）

Prepositional verbs always take a direct object, and the object must ALWAYS come after the preposition.
介系詞動詞後面一定要有直接受詞，並且受詞必須接於介系詞之後。

* I tend to **focus on** the details too much.
* I've **worked as** a hairdresser and a designer.
* I've been **waiting for** you for ages.
* I'm **looking for** a new job.

5 Fill in the blanks with the prepositions from the box.

| about | against | with | at |
| for | on | to | over |

1 I need to work _____ this report for a few more hours before I'm finished.

2 I've looked _____ your résumé, and it's very impressive.

3 What were we just talking _____? I've forgotten.

4 I'm sorry. I don't agree _____ you on that point.

5 May I ask _____ a glass of water?

6 What skills can you contribute _____ our company?

7 I'm sorry, but we decided _____ hiring you.

8 You must arrive _____ work on time every morning.

129

6 Role-Play! Choose one of the application forms below and use the questions to conduct an interview. Student A should play the interviewer, and student B should play the applicant.

1 Tell me a little bit about yourself and your education.
2 Tell me about your work experience.
3 Why should I hire you?
4 Do you _____ well? / Are you _____?
5 What's your biggest strength?
6 What's your biggest weakness?
7 Why do you want to work for this company?

APPLICATION FORM

Name Lewis Richards
From New York
Education
Athena University, BA in economics (2007-2011)
Work Experience
Researcher at Princeton Consulting (2011-2013)
Strengths
Attention to detail, organizational skills, time-management skills
Weaknesses
Working as part of a team
Reason for Applying Ready for a new challenge

APPLICATION FORM

Name Janet Poole
From London
Education
Warwick University, BA in art and design (2005-2008), MA in graphic design. (2008-2010)
Work Experience
Graphic designer at Sweep Design Solutions (2010-2011), project manager at Zeus Graphics (2011-2013)
Strengths
Creativity, handling responsibility, leadership skills
Weaknesses   **Reason for Applying**
Problem-solving skills   To show my true potential

7 Look at the picture sequences and use them to create dialogues.

| Example | Student A | Where do you see yourself in two years? |
| | Student B | In two years I'd like to be . . . |

A

 two years / team leader    long term / start own business   yearly salary / $30,000 ~ $40,000    work overtime / yes

B

 pay-range / $20,000 ~ $25,000    work weekends / prefer not to    five years / senior manager    10 years / CEO

VI. Now, Time to Pronounce!

Stress with Phrasal Verbs 短語動詞的重音

8 In phrasal verbs, the stress falls on the adverb, not the main verb. Listen and
172 repeat the following sentences. Pay attention to the stress on the phrasal verb.

> **1** **Where** did you <u>grow **up**</u>?
>
> **2** I **like** to <u>hang **out**</u> with my **friends**.
>
> **3** I **of**ten <u>get **up**</u> before **se**ven in the **mor**ning.
>
> **4** Can you **please** <u>check **over**</u> this re**port**?

173 ➡ BUT, when an object comes between the verb and the adverb, both parts are
often stressed. Listen and repeat.

> **1** I <u>**turned**</u> their **off**er <u>**down**</u>.
>
> **2** I **need** to <u>**think**</u> it <u>**over**</u> for a **while**.
>
> **3** Why don't you <u>**try**</u> it <u>**out**</u> for a **month**?
>
> **4** I **nev**er <u>**put**</u> **work** <u>**off**</u> until the **last mi**nute.

9 Look at the following sentences. Circle the words you think will receive stress.
174 Listen and check your answers. Then read the sentences aloud.

> **1** John thinks up new ideas all the time.
>
> **2** Do you pick things up quickly?
>
> **3** Don't give up yet.
>
> **4** Jane dropped out of college after a year.

Getting a Pet
養寵物

I. Topic Preview 🎧 175

1 Deciding what kind of pet to get 決定要養什麼寵物

We live in a small house, so maybe a small dog or a cat would be best.

But I'm allergic to cats, and I don't like dogs.

How about a fish, then?

Hmm, that's not a bad idea.

2 Describing the breed, history, and personality of a pet 描述寵物的品種、經歷和個性

Tell me about this dog.

He's a three-year-old male Labrador.

Has he been neutered?

Yes, he's already been neutered.

Why is he up for adoption?

He was abandoned by his owner.

What's his personality like?

He's very energetic and he loves people.

3 Asking how to take care of a certain pet 詢問如何照顧特定寵物

How often should we feed him?

You should feed him twice a day.

What brand of food would you recommend?

I'd recommend Happy Pup Dog Food.

4 Advising on long-term care 提出長期照顧的建議

When should we get him neutered?

You can get him neutered when he's six months old.

Is there anything else we should do?

You need to get him vaccinated annually.

II. Vocabulary & Phrases

Labrador 拉布拉多

Yorkshire terrier
約克夏梗犬

Birman 伯曼貓

ragdoll 布偶貓

mixed breed 混種

male 雄性　**female** 雌性

high/low maintenance
難／好照顧

abandon 棄養

adopt 領養

feed 餵食

walk (one's pet)
遛（寵物）

train (one's pet)
訓練（寵物）

get (one's pet) neutered / spayed
將（寵物）結紮

get (one's pet) tagged
讓（寵物）戴名牌

groom 打扮

get (one's pet) vaccinated
讓（寵物）注射預防針

Sentence Patterns

- *My husband* wants to get *a dog*, but *it's too much responsibility*.
  How about getting a *cat*? *Cats* are *pretty low maintenance*.
- If you get a *fish*, you have to *feed it*, *change its water* . . .
- *We* *aren't very active*, so maybe getting a *fish* would be best.
- Tell me about this *dog*.
  He's a *five*-year-old *male* *poodle*.
- Has *he* been *neutered*?

- Why is he/she up for adoption?
- What's his/her personality like?
  He/She is *great with kids* and *loves to cuddle*.
- How often should we *walk him*?
  You should *walk him* *twice a day*.
- What brand of food would you recommend?
  I'd recommend *Kitty Kat Cat Food*.
- When should we get him/her *vaccinated*?
  You can get him/her *vaccinated* when he/she is *six weeks* old.

III. Now, Time to Listen!

1 James and Fran are discussing which kind of pet to get. Listen to their conversation and check ☑ the correct answers.

178

1 Which of the following is NOT a reason why Fran doesn't want a dog?

- **a** ⃝ Dogs are not tidy.
- **b** ⃝ Dogs need exercise.
- **c** ⃝ Their house isn't big enough.

2 James
- **a** ⃝ doesn't like cats.
- **b** ⃝ is scared of cats.
- **c** ⃝ is allergic to cats.

3 Fran suggests getting
- **a** ⃝ a fish
- **b** ⃝ a rabbit
- **c** ⃝ a turtle

because they
- **a** ⃝ look and feel nice.
- **b** ⃝ are low maintenance.
- **c** ⃝ are good with children.

2 Tina is at the animal shelter talking to the manager about his cats. Listen to their conversation and fill in the profiles of the cats.

179

a
Name
_____
Gender _____
Age _____
❀❀❀❀❀❀❀❀
Personality
_____,
_____
Neutered/Spayed
_____
Vaccinated Yes
Other
_____ by
previous owner

b
Name
_____Sally_____
Gender _____
Age _____
❀❀❀❀❀❀❀❀
Personality
_____gentle_____,
_____playful_____
Neutered/Spayed
_____
Vaccinated _____
Other previous owner
didn't _____
_____

c
Name
_____
Gender M
Age _____ years
❀❀❀❀❀❀❀❀
Personality
_____,
loyal
Neutered/Spayed Yes
Vaccinated _____
Other
previous owner
_____

3 Now listen to the conversation Tina had with her friend earlier in the day. Check ☑ and write Tina's preferences.

180

Gender ☐ male ☐ female   Breed ☐ Birman ☐ ragdoll ☐ mixed
Age ☐ less than six months old ☐ more than six months old
Personality _____

Which pet do you think Tina will decide to adopt? ☐ Tom ☐ Sally ☐ Max

134

4 Use the pictures and context clues to fill in the blanks in the dialogues.
Use the words and phrases from the box.

I'd recommend	thinking of getting	change their water	twice a day would be	change it once every
often should I walk	too high maintenance	brand of fish food	make really good	Yorkshire terrier
golden retriever	feed them	is too small	pretty low maintenance	all you have to do
get a small dog	loyal and lots	get him neutered	is allergic to	be enough

A

Woman | So how often should I _____?

Man | You need to _____ two days.

Woman | And which _____

would you recommend?

Man | _____ Gold Medal.

B

Man | When can I _____?

Vet | Anytime after he's six months old.

Man | OK. And how _____ him?

Would once a day _____?

Vet | Hmm . . . for a big _____ like him,

_____ best.

C

Man | We're _____ a pet, but we're

not sure what to get.

Woman | How about getting a dog?

They're _____ of fun.

Man | I know, but our house _____.

Woman | You could _____, like a

_____.

Man | John doesn't like small dogs. He says they're

_____.

D

Man | I want a cat, but my wife _____ them.

Woman | That's a shame. Cats _____ pets.

Man | I know. They're _____ and really

affectionate.

Woman | What about a hamster? They're cute, and

_____ is _____

and clean out their cage.

Man | That's a pretty good idea.

181 ➔ Now listen and check your answers.

IV. Now, Grammar Time!

Adjective-Preposition Combinations
形容詞與介系詞的組合

scared tired + of fond	responsible grateful + for sorry	good bored + with familiar	allergic similar + to mean

5 Fill the blanks in the following sentences with an adjective-preposition combination.

1 I'm _____ cats because one scratched me when I was a kid.

2 Labradors are supposed to be really _____ children.

3 Get a pet? I just don't know if I can be _____ another living creature.

4 He's _____ dog hair. He sneezes if he gets too close to a dog.

5 I'm really _____ you helping me find such a great pet!

6 I'm so _____ my dog barking. He just won't stop!

7 I'm really _____ cats. I have seven of them altogether.

8 You're right. Sphinxes do look quite _____ Oriental shorthairs.

Phrasal-Prepositional Verbs
(verb + adverb + preposition)
片語介系詞動詞（動詞+副詞+介系詞）

Phrasal-prepositional verbs always take a direct object, and the object must ALWAYS come after the preposition.
片語介系詞動詞一定要接直接受詞，受詞也必須置於介系詞之後。

- Ragdolls are really friendly. They **get along with** children really well.
- I'm so excited! I'm really **looking forward to** getting my new dog.
- We need to go to the pet store. We've almost **run out of** turtle food.
- I could never get a dog. I just couldn't **put up with** the barking.

➡ Here are some more phrasal-prepositional verbs. Look up their meanings in your dictionary and make sentences with your partner.

| come down with | grow out of | look out for | get away with | get around to |

6 Correct the mistakes in the following sentences.

1 I need to take my cat to get neutered, but I haven't got around it to yet.

_____

2 My puppy always goes to the bathroom on the carpet. I hope he'll run out of it soon.

_____

3 My cat Minx is quite short-tempered, so she doesn't get away with other cats very well.

_____

4 We'd better take Pickle to the vet. I think she's come something down with.

_____

5 I think it's important for owners and their pets to put out for each other.

_____

V. Now, Time to Speak!

More Cat and Dog Breeds
更多犬貓品種

corgi
柯基犬

red toy poodle
紅貴賓

golden retriever
黃金獵犬

Scottish fold
蘇格蘭摺耳貓

sphynx
加拿大無毛貓

Oriental shorthair
東方短毛貓

7 Pair Work! Follow the arrows and ask and answer the questions.

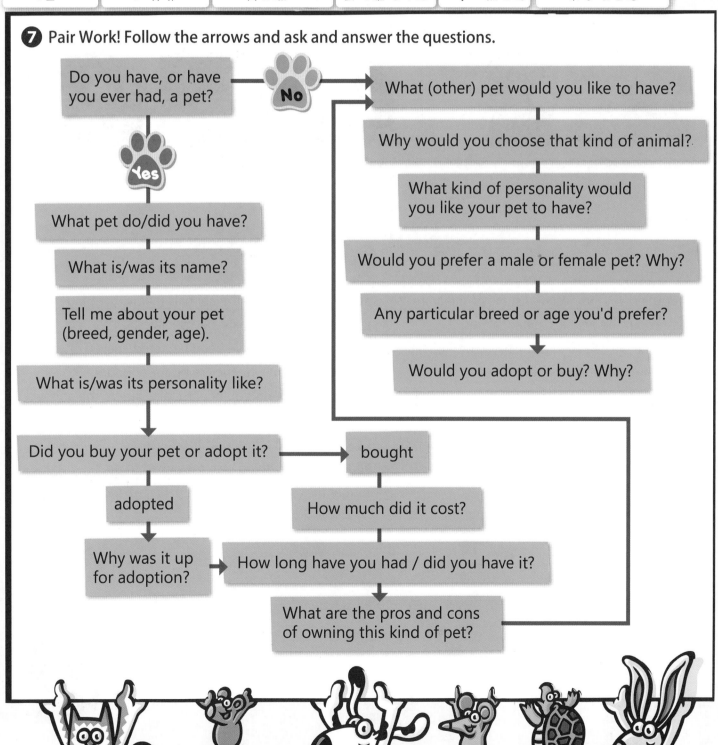

Do you have, or have you ever had, a pet?

No → What (other) pet would you like to have?

Why would you choose that kind of animal?

What kind of personality would you like your pet to have?

Would you prefer a male or female pet? Why?

Any particular breed or age you'd prefer?

Would you adopt or buy? Why?

Yes

What pet do/did you have?

What is/was its name?

Tell me about your pet (breed, gender, age).

What is/was its personality like?

Did you buy your pet or adopt it? → bought

How much did it cost?

adopted

Why was it up for adoption? → How long have you had / did you have it?

What are the pros and cons of owning this kind of pet?

8 Role-Play! Student A should play someone who wants to adopt one of the animals at the bottom of this page. Student B should play the owner of an animal shelter. Use the prompts and pictures to create a conversation.

Adjectives describing an animal's personality
形容動物個性的用語 🐾

loving 惹人愛的

affectionate 熱情的

shy 害羞的

gentle 溫馴的

energetic 好動的

lively 活潑的

grumpy 乖戾的

loyal 忠心的

playful 愛玩的

relaxed 懶洋洋的

Student A
(someone who wants to adopt an animal)

1 Ask the owner to describe some of the animals.

2 Ask about the animals' personalities.

3 Ask if they've been neutered/spayed or vaccinated.

4 Ask why they're up for adoption.

5 Choose an animal you'd like to adopt.
Ask how often you should feed/walk/groom it.

6 Ask what brand of food he/she'd recommend.

7 Ask if there's anything else you should do.

Student B
(animal shelter owner)

1 Describe some of the animals (name, breed, gender, age).

2 Describe the animals' personalities.

3 Say whether they've been neutered/spayed or vaccinated.

4 Give a reason why they're up for adoption.

5 Advise Student B on how to take care of the animal.

6 Recommend a brand of food.

7 Tell them anything else they need to do
(get the animal vaccinated, *neutered, tagged, etc.).*

Foo-Foo

Elizabeth

Baldy

Midnight

VI. Now, Time to Pronounce!

Starting Pitch 發語音調

High starting pitch 高發語音調

A high starting pitch means that the speaker intends to express a different opinion to what has just been said or is changing the topic.
發語時提高音調，表示説話者對於對方説的話持有不同的看法，或者想要轉移話題。

9 Listen to the short dialogue, paying attention to the starting pitches throughout.

182

Chat   ...

Kim: I think cats are really cool animals.

Remy: I hate cats! I think they're really bad-tempered.

Kim: Dogs, on the other hand, are really annoying.

Remy: You're so wrong. Having a dog is the best!

Write a message   Send

➡ Now practice the conversation with a partner.

Low starting pitch 低發語音調

A low starting pitch shows that a piece of information is simply extra detail and not meant to change the topic. Think of the information as being in brackets. 發語時降低音調，表示説話者只是要額外補充一些資訊，並沒有要轉移話題，把這些資訊假想成括弧補充，就很容易理解。

10 Listen to the short dialogue, paying attention to the starting pitches throughout.

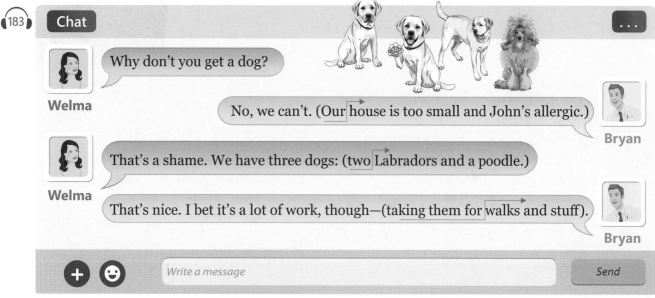

183

Chat   ...

Welma: Why don't you get a dog?

Bryan: No, we can't. (Our house is too small and John's allergic.)

Welma: That's a shame. We have three dogs: (two Labradors and a poodle.)

Bryan: That's nice. I bet it's a lot of work, though—(taking them for walks and stuff).

Write a message   Send

英語力 3

16堂流利英語聽說訓練課

Listening and Speaking in Everyday Life

作　　者	Owain Mckimm
翻　　譯	丁宥榆
英文審訂	Treva Adams
企劃編輯	葉俞均
校　　對	歐寶妮
編　　輯	王鈺婷
內文排版	蔡怡柔／丁宥榆
封面設計	林書玉
圖　　片	Shutterstock
製程管理	洪巧玲
發 行 人	黃朝萍
出 版 者	寂天文化事業股份有限公司
電　　話	+886-(0)2-2365-9739
傳　　真	+886-(0)2-2365-9835
網　　址	www.icosmos.com.tw
讀者服務	onlineservice@icosmos.com.tw
出版日期	2024 年 5 月 初版一刷（寂天雲隨身聽 APP 版）

英語力 . 3：16 堂流利英語聽說訓練課（寂天雲隨身
聽 APP）/ Owain Mckimm 作；丁宥榆譯 . -- 初版 . --
[臺北市]：寂天文化，2024.05
　面；　公分

ISBN 978-626-300-251-7（菊 8K）
1.CST: 英語 2.CST: 讀本

805.18　　　　　　　　　　　　　113005315